Oliver Optic

All Aboard

Or, life on the lake.

Oliver Optic

All Aboard
Or, life on the lake.

ISBN/EAN: 9783337413279

Printed in Europe, USA, Canada, Australia, Japan

Cover: Foto ©Andreas Hilbeck / pixelio.de

More available books at **www.hansebooks.com**

ALL ABOARD;

OR,

LIFE ON THE LAKE.

A SEQUEL TO "THE BOAT CLUB."

BY

OLIVER OPTIC.

BOSTON:
LEE AND SHEPARD,
(SUCCESSORS TO PHILLIPS, SAMPSON & CO.)
1870.

TO

MY NEPHEW,

ABRAHAM MITCHELL JR.,

This Book

IS AFFECTIONATELY DEDICATED

THE BOAT CLUB SERIES.

THE BOAT CLUB; or, THE BUNKERS OF RIPPLETON.

ALL ABOARD; or, LIFE ON THE LAKE.

NOW OR NEVER; or, THE ADVENTURES OF BOBBY BRIGHT.

LITTLE BY LITTLE; or, THE CRUISE OF THE FLYAWAY.

TRY AGAIN; or, THE TRIALS AND TRIUMPHS OF HARRY WEST.

POOR AND PROUD; or, THE FORTUNES OF KATY REDBURN.

PREFACE.

"ALL ABOARD" was written to gratify the reasonable curiosity of the readers of "THE BOAT CLUB" to know what occurred at Wood Lake during the second season; and, though it is a sequel, it has no direct connection with its predecessor. The Introduction, in the first chapter, contains a brief synopsis of the principal events of the first season; so that those who have not read "The Boat Club," will labor under no disadvantage on that account.

The *story* of each book is entirely distinct from that of the other. As the interest of the first centres in Tony Weston, so that of the second does in Charles Hardy. I have tried to make the boys believe that the path of truth and rectitude is not only the safest, but the pleasantest path; and the

1 *   (5)

experience of Charles with the "Rovers" illustrates and supports the position.

Perhaps some of the older readers of these books will think that, in providing the boys at Wood Lake with a whole fleet of boats, with bands of music, with club rooms, libraries, and apparatus, I have furnished them with very magnificent recreations; and that I might as well have told a "fairy tale" while I was about it. The only excuse I can offer for this extravagance is, that it would have been a pity to spoil a splendid ideal, when it could be actualized by a single stroke of the pen; besides, I believe that nothing is too good for good boys, especially when it is paid for out of the pocket of a *millionnaire.*

The author, grateful to his young friends for the kind reception given to "The Boat Club," hopes that "All Aboard" will not only please them, but make them wiser and better.

WILLIAM T. ADAMS.

DORCHESTER, October 25, 1855.

CONTENTS.

CHAPTER   PAGE

I. INTRODUCTION 11

II. THE NEW MEMBER 18

III. ALL ABOARD 33

IV. THE FRATERNAL HUG 47

V. UP THE RIVER 59

VI. HURRAH FOR TONY 71

VII. COMMODORE FRANK SEDLEY . . . 84

VIII. THE RACE 96

IX. LITTLE PAUL 109

X. A UNANIMOUS VOTE 122

XI. BETTER TO GIVE THAN RECEIVE . . 134

XII. FIRST OF MAY 144

(7)

XIII. THE LIGHTHOUSE. 159

XIV. THE CONSPIRACY. 171

XV. THE ROVERS. 183

XVI. THE CAMP ON THE ISLAND. . . . 195

XVII. THE ESCAPE. 209

XVIII. WRECK OF THE BUTTERFLY. . . . 221

XIX. THE CRUISE OF THE FLEET. . . . 232

XX. THE HOSPITALITIES OF OAKLAWN. . 244

XXI. CONCLUSION. 254

ALL ABOARD.

ALL ABOARD;

OR,

LIFE ON THE LAKE.

CHAPTER I.

INTRODUCTION.

IT can hardly be supposed that all the boys who take up this book have read the Boat Club; therefore it becomes necessary, before the old friends of the club are permitted to reunite with them, to introduce whatever new friends may be waiting to join them in the sports of the second season at Wood Lake. However wearisome such a presentation may be to those who are already acquainted, my young friends will all allow that it is nothing more than civility and good manners.

Frank Sedley is the only son of Captain Sedley, a retired shipmaster, of lofty and liberal views, and of the most estimable character. He is not what some people would call an "old fogy," and likes to have the boys enjoy themselves in every thing that is reasonable and proper; but not to the detriment of their manners or morals, or to the neglect of their usual duties.

Having been a sailor all his life, he has none of that fear of boats and deep water which often haunts the minds of fond parents, and has purchased a beautiful club boat for the use of his son and other boys who live in the vicinity of Wood Lake.

Some fathers and mothers may think this was a very foolish act on the part of Captain Sedley; that the amusement he had chosen for his son was too dangerous in itself, and too likely to create in him a taste for aquatic pursuits that may one day lead him to be a sailor, which some tender mothers regard as "a dreadful thing," as, indeed, it is, under some circumstances.

But it must be remembered that Captain Sedley had been a sailor himself; that he had followed the seas from early youth; and that he had made his fortune and earned his reputation as a wise, good, and respectable man, on the sea. So, of course, he could not sympathize with the general opinion that a ship must necessarily be a "sink of iniquity," a school of vice, and that nothing good can be expected of a boy who is sent to sea. He believes that the man will grow out of the boy; and to his parental duty he applies the apostolic maxim, "Whatsoever a man soweth, that shall he also reap."

The club boat and the boat club, as means of instruction and discipline, as well as of amusement, were suggested by an accidental occurrence. The "Bunkers of Rippleton," a set of idle and dissolute boys, had constructed a rude raft, upon which they paddled about on the lake, and appeared to enjoy themselves very much. Captain Sedley, who had forbidden his son to venture upon the lake on the raft, or ⸺on in a boat, without permission, overheard Charles ⸺ly, the intimate friend of Frank, remark that the "Bunkers" had a much better time than they had, and that boys who did not obey their parents often enjoyed themselves more than those who did.

2

A. few days after, the boys discovered the club boat, the light and graceful Zephyr, resting like a fairy shell upon the lake, and in its use the argument of Charles was effectually refuted. A club was formed of the boys in the neighborhood, and under the instruction of Uncle Ben, an old sailor who lived with Captain Sedley, soon became very expert in the management of the boat. A building was erected for the use of the association, in which, besides the boat house, was a club room containing a library, and furnished with conveniences for holding meetings for mutual instruction and recreation. A constitution for the government of the club was adopted, in which the object of the association was declared to be "the instruction and amusement of the members, and the acquiring of good morals, good manners, and good habits in general." It defined and prohibited a great many vices and bad habits common among boys, so that the tendency of the organization was to make them better, wiser, and happier.

Their experience upon the lake, while the influence of the association stimulated them to the strict performance of their ordinary duties, was both varied and useful. Inasmuch as it reduced their recreation to a system, the laws of the club acting as a salutary check upon the waywardness of youth, it afforded an excellent discipline for the mind and heart, as well as for the muscles.

Among the members of the club was an honest, noble-hearted youth, the son of a poor widow, by the name of Tony Weston. In an affray upon Centre Island, Tony had taken the part of Frank Sedley against Tim Bunker, and had thus obtained the ill will of the leader of the "Bunkers," and is accused of stealing a wallet, which is afterwards proved to have been taken by the "Bunker" himself. The theft is proved upon the graceless scamp, and he is sent to the house of correction, while Tony is borne in triumph by the club to his home.

Near the close of the story, Tony's brother, who has long been mourned as dead, returns home from California, with a large fortune in his possession. The brother, George Weston, builds a fine house for his mother, and, impelled by a warm admiration for Tony's noble character, purchases a splendid club boat for him, of the size and model of the Zephyr, which is named the Butterfly.

Tony is a boy whom all my readers will like, and though he is really no better boy than Frank Sedley, the humble circumstances of his mother before George returned required a great deal of sacrifice on his part, and called into action a great many noble traits of character. His life was a struggle, and his character a triumph over the perils to which poverty exposed him.

His experience seemed to exemplify the truths of Christianity. He could forgive his enemy, as when, at the risk of his own life, he plunged into the lake and rescued Tim Bunker from a watery grave, though Tim was even then laboring to ruin him. He loved to sacrifice his own comfort to that of others, and found his greatest pleasure in making others happy. He and Frank are the unconscious exemplars of the boat club — the " men of character and influence " in their embryo world.

Charles Hardy is a boy of another stamp — one who does things " to be seen of men." He is sometimes selfish and ambitious; though the beneficent influence of the organization is working miracles in the transformation of his character.

The Butterfly was launched in the month of April. The liberality of George Weston had provided for her a boat house, similar to that of the Zephyr, and, like that, furnished with a club room and library, and all the means for promoting the objects of the organization.

And now, with my old friends refreshed in memory by this review of the first season, and my new ones put in possession of all that is necessary to a proper understanding of the situation of the boat club, we are ready to proceed with our story.

2*

CHAPTER II.

THE NEW MEMBER.

"ORDER!" said Frank Sedley, as he seated himself in the arm chair, at the head of the table in the club room.

At a meeting the preceding week, Frank had again been chosen coxswain of the club for the first official term. This had been done, not only in compliment to the noble boy to whose father the members were indebted for the privileges they enjoyed, but in anticipation of an exciting time on the lake, in a proposed race with the Butterfly. Frank was acknowledged to be the most skilful boatman among them, and under his direction they expected to accomplish all that they and the Zephyr could possibly attain. They had already learned that mere muscle was not all that was required to insure their success. Skill, forethought, and the ability to take advantage of favoring circumstances, were discovered to be even more desirable than great power.

"Order!" repeated Frank, rapping smartly on the table.

The members suspended their conversation, and all eyes were fixed upon the president. The affairs of the club, in connection with the Butterfly, had been freely discussed for several weeks, and every thing had been arranged for the opening of the "summer campaign," as Charles Hardy rather facetiously called it

"There are two questions to be submitted for the action of the club at this meeting," continued Frank, with more than his usual gravity. "They are questions of momentous consequence, and I have felt the need of counsel from our director; but my father declines giving me any advice, and says he prefers that we should discuss the questions independently; though, as you all know, if our final action is wrong, he will — he will —— "

"Veto it," added Fred Harper.

"Yes; he will not permit us to do a wrong, though he wants us to think for ourselves, and do the best we can."

" Precisely so; he wants ——" Charles Hardy began.

" Order ! " said Frank, with gentle firmness. " The first question is this : Tim Bunker, who has recently been discharged from the house of correction, has applied to be admitted as a member of the club, in place of Tony Weston, resigned. Shall he be admitted ? "

" Mr. President, I move that he be not admitted," said Charles.

" Is the motion seconded ? "

There was no response. The members all felt that it was a very delicate matter, and that it required careful deliberation.

" The motion is not seconded, and, of course, cannot be entertained," continued the president.

" I move that he be admitted," said Fred Harper.

" Second the motion," added William Bright.

Charles Hardy felt a little nettled, and his first impulse was, to rise and express his astonishment, as Squire Flutter had done in the " March meeting," at the motion of his friend on the other side of the table : but the impulsive youth had learned quite recently that a second thought is oftentimes much better than a first, and he reserved the expression of his surprise till a later stage of the debate.

As no one seemed disposed to open the discussion, Frank requested Fred Harper to take the chair, while he temporarily assumed the position of one of the disputants.

"Mr. Chairman," said he, "I rise to offer a few remarks in favor of the motion which is now before the club. Perhaps I cannot better introduce my own views upon the subject than by relating the substance of the conversation that occurred when Tim applied to me for admission to the club. He said that he had had a hard time of it in the house of correction; but he hoped his long confinement had done him good. He had firmly resolved to be a good boy. 'But,' said he, 'what can I do? If I go with the fellows I used to associate with, how can I keep my resolution? I know I have been a very bad boy, and I want to do what is right.' I told him that our rules were very strict; that no fellow was allowed to swear or to use bad language of any kind; and that every member was required to keep straight himself,

and help keep the others straight. He would agree
to all this, would sign the constitution, and my father
and the club would soon see that he meant all he
said. I confess that I felt for him. What he said
about keeping company with the ' Bunkers ' — I suppose we must drop that name now — was true. He
could not be a good fellow with such as they are.
Now, it won't do any harm to try him, and he may
be saved from the error of his ways. As it is, he
has got a hard name, and people will shun him; and,
being discouraged, he may plunge deeper into vice
than ever. This is about all I have to say."

Frank resumed the chair, and several of the members, perceiving the force of the president's reasoning,
expressed themselves in favor of admitting Tim;
when Charles Hardy rose, and " plumed himself for
a speech."

" Mr. President: I confess my surprise at the
direction this debate has taken. There's a *destiny*
that shapes our ends ——"

" A what?" asked Fred Harper, with a roguish
smile.

" I beg the member on the other side will not interrupt me," replied Charles, with offended dignity. "I quote the line as John Adams used it, in his celebrated speech, ' Sink or swim.' "

"Who?"

"John Adams."

"I beg the member's pardon, but John Adams never made any such speech," answered Fred, who, it must be confessed, was rather too fond of tantalizing the ambitious youth.

"Really, Mr. President, I am surprised that the member should deny what we all know. Why, the piece is in our reading book."

"Daniel Webster put the speech into the mouth of Adams," added Frank; "and the patriot is only supposed to have made it."

"It amounts to the same thing," continued Charles, with a slight blush.

"But your quotation was not correct," said Fred.

"Perhaps the member will give me the correct reading of the passage."

"With pleasure; the lines are from Shakspeare:—

' There's a Divinity that shapes our ends,
Roughhew them as we will.'

I fancy the lines will not suit the member now," continued Fred, as he cast a mischievous glance at the discomfited speech-maker.

"Go on, if you please," said Frank to Charles.

"As I was saying, Mr. President, 'There's a Divinity that shapes our ends' ——"

"You were not saying so," interposed Fred.

"Order!" said the chairman. "Proceed."

But Charles Hardy could not proceed. Undoubtedly, when he rose to speak, he had an idea in his head; but it had fled, and he could not at once recall it. In vain he scratched his head, in vain he thrust his hands into his pockets, as if in search of the lost idea; it would not come.

"You were speaking of Tim Bunker," said Frank, suggestively.

"I was; and I was about to say that — that ——"

Some of the boys could no longer suppress their mirth, and, in spite of the vigorous pounding which the chairman bestowed upon the innocent table, in his attempts to preserve order, they had their laugh out. But the pleasantry of the members, and a sense of the awkwardness of his position, roused Charles

to a more vigorous effort, and, as he was about to
speak of another topic, the lost idea came like a flood
of sunshine.

"'There's a Divinity that shapes our ends.' Tim
Bunker has chosen the path he will tread, and does
any body suppose he will ever abandon it? He will
certainly die in the State Prison or on the gallows —
my father says so. We all know what his habits
are, and it is as easy for an Ethiopian to change his
spots ——"

"Skin," said Fred.

"To change his skin, as for such a fellow to be
like us. He will lie, swear, ——"

"The chair thinks the member's remarks are not
strictly in order," interposed Frank, who was much
pained to hear his friend use such violent language.

He saw that Charles was smarting under the effects
of the ridicule which his companions had cast upon
him, and that, in his struggle to make a speech, and
thus redeem himself from the obloquy of a failure,
he had permitted his impulses to override his judgment.

"I forbear, then," continued the speaker. "But

3

I beg tne club to consider the probable consequences of admitting such a fellow into the association. We have thus far enjoyed a good reputation, and we ought to be very careful how we tamper with our respectability."

" Ahem ! " said Fred.

" Order ! "

" A good name is rather to be chosen than — than *purple and fine linen.*"

" Than what ! " exclaimed Fred.

" Great riches," added Frank, with a smile, and even he was forced to admit " that the member was singularly unfortunate in his quotations."

" You have my opinion, gentlemen," said Charles, " and I don't know that I have any thing more to say at present ; " and, much disconcerted, he sat down.

But though cast down, he was not destroyed ; and in justice to his companions, it must be remarked that he had frequently annoyed the club by his attempts to make speeches more learned and ornate than his capacity would allow. Frank had reasoned with him on this propensity to " show off," but without effect, so that he did not feel so much sympathy for him at the present time as he would have felt under other circumstances.

"The question is still open for discussion," said the chairman.

No one, however, seemed disposed to speak.

"Question!" called Fred Harper.

"Question!" repeated several others.

"Are you ready for the question?" continued the chairman.

"Question!"

"All those in favor of admitting Tim Bunker as a member of the club will signify it in the usual way."

Ten hands were raised.

"Contrary minded."

Charles, feeling that he was on the wrong side, did not vote against the measure, and it was declared to be a unanimous vote.

"The other matter, requiring the action of the club, relates to the proposed race between the Butterfly and the Zephyr. Several gentlemen of Rippleton feel a deep interest in the two boat clubs, and have proposed to put up a prize to be awarded to the successful club. I understand that fifty dollars have been subscribed for this purpose. The question is, Shall we pull for this prize?"

" When ?" asked Fred.

" The clubs may choose their own time."

" It wouldn't be fair till the Butterfly has had a chance to practise a while."

" Of course not; the Butterfly may accept the proposition or not, and the club can select their own time."

" I move you that the offer be accepted," said William Bright.

" Second the motion," added James Vincent.

" I make the motion, Mr. President, for the purpose of bringing the question properly before the club. I have not thought enough about the matter yet to decide whether I am in favor of it or not," continued William Bright.

" It is generally supposed that the one who makes a motion is in favor of it; but we won't mind that now," said Frank, with a smile.

" Mr. President, I must say, I think the proposition looks a little like gambling," suggested Charles Hardy.

"So I was thinking," added a little fellow, near the foot of the table.

"Suppose we take an informal vote," proposed Charles, who was determined to get on the right side this time, if possible.

So an informal vote *was* taken, and every member voted against the proposition.

Frank Sedley was surprised at this result. Probably he was the only one who had given any earnest thought to the subject, though the offer was known to all the boys.

Captain Sedley, who watched over the welfare of the club with paternal interest, had endeavored, during the winter that was now past, to render it effectual in developing the moral and mental capacities of the members. He had given such a direction to the exercises in Zephyr Hall as he thought would best attain this end. One of the greatest difficulties with which he had been obliged to contend was the want of individuality in the boys. Each was disposed to "pin his faith" upon others. They would not think for themselves, and exercise an independent judgment. Like thousands in the great world, they

3 *

" went with the crowd ;" thought, acted, voted, with the majority.

Frank saw the operation of this motive in the "informal vote" which had just been taken ; and he was tolerably certain that he could bring them all over to the other side, by indicating his own preference.

Calling Fred Harper to the chair again, he opened the discussion by offering a simile, which, being a parallel case, certainly gave the question an entirely new aspect.

"At the Rippleton Academy three gold medals and three silver medals are awarded, every year, for the best scholarship and deportment. Is that gambling ? "

" No," replied half a dozen voices.

" Well, we are to row, in like manner, for a prize. We don't put up money as a stake; the party that gets beaten does not lose any thing."

" That makes a difference," added Charles.

" But the prizes in the Academy are given to make the scholars get their lessons well — to stimulate them in doing their duty," said William Bright

" Very true ; " and Frank saw, in the faces of the members, that the current had again set in another direction. " But we only want to prove that rowing for the prize is not gambling."

" That's all," said Charles.

" The Agricultural Society offers premiums for the best horses, cows, oxen."

" That's to improve stock," answered William. " Boat racing can only be for amusement."

" The Horticultural Society gives premiums for the prettiest flowers," added Frank ; " and my father got one of them last summer."

The boys were staggered again.

" Flowers are cultivated for amusement ; at any rate, we don't eat them, or drink them, or sleep on them," continued Frank.

" Your bed shall be roses, besprinkled with dew,"

tdded Fred, who never missed his joke. " Besides, we sleep on poppies. They are a sleepy plant, you know."

" But the real question, ' said Frank, " is, whether racing for a prize will not excite hard and envious

feelings in the members of the two clubs. I hope
we shall think well of it before we vote; and for that
purpose, Mr. Chairman, I move a recess of half an
hour."

The motion was carried, and the boys talked the
matter over till the meeting was called to order
again.

"Question!" called several voices.

The vote was immediately taken, and it stood nine
in favor and two opposed to the proposition. And
so, on the part of the Zephyr, the offer was accepted.

The club then adjourned for an excursion on the
lake.

CHAPTER III.

ALL ABOARD!

THE club had taken their seats in the boats, and were waiting the orders of the coxswain to haul her out of her berth, when Captain Sedley made his appearance.

"You are short-handed, Frank," said he, as he observed Tony's vacant seat.

"Yes, sir; but we have elected a member to fill that place," replied Frank, as he jumped out of the boat, and hastened to inform his father of what the club had done.

The members all felt a deep interest in the result of this conference; and though this was the first excursion of the season, they forgot for the time the pleasure before them in their desire to know whether the "director" would approve their action in relation to the new member and the prize.

Frank and his father entered the club room together.

"Now, my son, what have you done?" asked Captain Sedley.

"We have discussed both questions to the best of our ability," replied Frank, with some hesitation.

"Well, what was the result?"

"We have elected Tim to fill Tony's place."

"Indeed!"

"We have; and we await your sanction to our doings."

"Did you think I would sanction such a choice as that?"

"I didn't know. We have fairly considered the matter; have faithfully examined both sides of the question. If we have done wrong, you know, father, that you have a veto upon our doings."

Captain Sedley smiled at the matter-of-fact, business-like earnestness of his son. He felt quite as much interest in the action of the boys as they did to learn his opinion of it.

"Tim is a very bad boy," said he.

"He *was;* but he has solemnly promised to amend, and become a good boy," answered Frank, warmly.

"Not much dependence can be placed upon the promises of such boys as Tim."

"But if no one encourages him to become better, he will not be likely to improve much, especially when every body despises and shuns him."

"There is danger that he may corrupt the rest of the club."

"He must obey the requirements of the constitution, or he cannot long continue to be a member."

"You are right, Frank ; I approve your action in this matter, but I should like to know the grounds upon which you admitted him."

Frank gave him a brief synopsis of the debate, and the anxious father expressed himself well pleased with the liberal views of the club.

"Men might be oftener reformed in the great world, if people would only give them a chance to be respectable, as you have done with Tim," said Captain Sedley. "But what have you done about the prize ?"

"We have voted to accept the offer of the gentlemen," answered Frank, rather doubtfully, as he looked earnestly into the face of his father, to discover the effect of his intelligence.

"I hope you looked on both sides of this question, as well as the other."

"We did, father."

Frank stated the different opinions that had been expressed by the members during the debate, and the fact that they had informally given a unanimous vote against it. Captain Sedley was much amused by the narration, in spite of the disappointment he felt at the ill success of his efforts to make the boys reason for themselves.

"I think your view is correct, Frank; though I am aware that many mature minds would arrive at a different conclusion. As you say, the envy and ill will which the contest may excite are the evils most to be dreaded."

"Then you approve our decision?"

"I do."

Frank felt as happy at that moment as though he had been a general of division, and had won a great victory. The consciousness of having arrived, unaided by mature minds, at a correct conclusion, was a triumph in itself. He had exercised his thought, and it had borne him to a right judgment. He was proud of his achievement, and hastened back to the boat with the intelligence of the approval.

"What does he say?" asked half a dozen of the members.

"Let us get off first, and then we will talk about it," replied Frank. "Bowman, let go the painter; cast off the stern lines, there. Now, back her — steady."

"Tell us about it, Frank," said Charles Hardy, as the Zephyr glided clear of the boat house, out upon the deep waters of the lake.

"Ready — up!" continued Frank, and the eleven oars were poised perpendicularly in the air.

"Down!"

The members had already begun to feel the inspiration of their favorite amusement, and there appeared to have been nothing lost by the season of inactivity which had passed away. They were as prompt and as perfect in the drill as though they had practised it every day during the winter. Although it was a moment of excitement, there was no undue haste ; every member seemed to be perfectly cool.

" Ready — pull ! "

And the broad blades dipped in the water, and bent before the vigorous arms of the youthful oarsmen.

" Starboard oars, cease rowing — back ! " continued the coxswain, with admirable dignity and self-posses-sion ; and the Zephyr, acted upon by this manœu-vre, came about as though upon a pivot, without going either backward or forward.

" Starboard oars, steady — pull ! " and the rowers indicated by this command caught the stroke, and the light bark shot ahead, with her wonted speed, in the direction of Rippleton village.

" Zephyr, ahoy ! " shouted some one from the shore.

" Tim Bunker — ain't it ? " asked Charles.

" Yes."

" Humph ! he needn't hail us like that. I was sure your father would never permit him to join the club," continued Charles, who fancied that he read in Frank's expression the disapproval of his father.

" You are in the wrong, Charley."

" Am I ? "

" You are; my father cordially approved our action. Now, Zephyrs, I am going up to Flat Rock to take him aboard; and I hope every fellow will treat him well — just as though he had never done any thing out of the way. What do you say ? "

" We will," they replied, with one voice.

" And then, if he does not walk straight, it will not be our fault. Treat him as though he was the best fellow among us. Let nothing tempt us to forget it."

Frank headed the boat towards the rock in the grove, and in a moment the bow touched it.

Without waiting for an invitation, Tim jumped into the boat, and took the vacant seat. Frank did not much like this forwardness; it was a little too " brazen " to comport with his ideas of true penitence. But he did not care to humble the " Bunker ; " so he said nothing that would wound his feelings.

" We are glad to see you, Tim; the club has this day elected you a member, and our director has approved the vote," said Frank.

Has he ? " replied Tim. with a broad grin.

" And, if you like, we will go up to the bot
house, where you may sign the constitution."

" Yes, I'll sign it," answered Tim, more as though
it would be conferring a favor on the club than as a
duty he owed to his new friends.

Frank gave the necessary orders to get the boat
under way again. Tim handled his oar with considerable skill, and before they reached the boat-house,
he had learned to time his stroke with that of his
companions.

When they landed, Captain Sedley took Tim apart
with him, and very kindly told him what would be
expected of him in his new relation, urging him to
be true to his good resolution, and assuring him that
he should never want for substantial encouragement
so long as he persevered in well doing. Tim hung
his head down while he listened to this kind advice ;
his answers were short, but they were all satisfactory,
so far as words could be taken as the index of his
intentions.

Frank then read the constitution, and the new
member listened to it with attention. The stringent
provisions of the sixth article, which forbade swear-

ing, indecent language, and other boyish vices, brought a scarcely visible smile to his lips, and excited a doubt as to the success of the experiment in the mind of the director

" Now, Tim, you can sign it," said Frank.

"It's pretty strict — ain't it?" added Tim, with one of his peculiar grins, as he took the pen that was handed to him. "You know I ain't used to being quite so strained up as you fellers, and I may kinder break through afore I know it."

"If you do, you shall be judged kindly and charitably," said Captain Sedley.

"Well, I'll sign it."

But it was not quite so easy a thing for Tim to sign; at least, to perform the mechanical part of the act, for he had been to school but little, and good penmanship was not one of his accomplishments. However, he succeeded in getting over the form, though it would have puzzled the secretary to read t, if he had not known what it was.

"Now, Zephyrs, Tim is one of us," said Frank.

"He hasn't got any uniform," suggested Charles.

"He shall have one " replied Captain Sedley, as

4 *

he wrote an order on Mr. Burlap, the tailor, to sup-
ply him with a uniform.

"All aboard!" shouted Frank. "We will pull
up the lake, and see how the Butterfly gets along.
They have been practising for a fortnight, and they
ought to be able to row pretty well by this time."

"With Uncle Ben to show them how," added
Fred Harper.

Again the Zephyrs were in their seats, and the
boat was backed out into the lake. The flags were
unrolled, and put in their places. The graceful barge
was nicely trimmed, so as to rest exactly square in
the water, and every thing was ready for a sharp
pull. The weather was cool, and the boys required
some pretty vigorous exercise to keep them warm.

The various commands were given, and executed
with the usual precision, only that Tim, who was not
thoroughly "broken in," made some blunders, though,
considering his short service, his proficiency was decidedly creditable.

The Zephyr darted away like an arrow, and the
slow, measured, musical stroke of the oars was
pleasant and exciting to the rowers.

" You haven't told us about the other matter **yet,** Frank," said Charles, as the boat skimmed along over the little waves of the lake.

" Let us know about it," added Fred.

" About what ? " asked Tim Bunker, whose modesty in his new position did not seem to cause **him** much trouble.

" We are to have a race with the Butterfly, when Tony gets things to his mind," replied Frank.

" That'll be fun ! Are ye going to put up **any** thing ? "

" Put up any thing ? "

" Yes ; what's going to be the stakes ? "

" I don't know what you mean, Tim."

" When they race hosses, each man bets on **his** own."

" We are not going to bet ; that would be contrary to the constitution."

" Would it ? I didn't hear nothing about betting."

" Article second says that one of the objects of the association shall be the acquiring of good habits in general ; and I am sure betting is a very bad habit.'

" Well, I s'pose it is."

" But several gentlemen of Rippleton have subscribed fifty dollars as a prize to the winner of the
race," added Frank; " just as they give medals in
school, you know."

" Well, of course you will win."

" I don't know."

" You are used to your boat, and them fellers
ain't."

" We can't tell yet; perhaps the Butterfly will
prove to be a faster boat than the Zephyr, and some
of Tony's members are a good deal larger and stouter
than ours.   I think the chances are about equal."

" I think likely.   What you going to do with the
money if you win ? "

" I don't know ; we haven't thought of that yet,"
replied Frank, not particularly pleased with the
question.

" Divide it among the fellers, I s'pose."

" I think not ; we had better apply it to some
useful purpose, — that is, if we win it, — such as enlarging our library, buying some philosophical instru-
ments ——"

"What's them?"

"An air pump, and other apparatus of the kind."

Tim did not comprehend the nature of the mystical implements any better than before; but as his mind was fixed upon something else, he did not demand further explanation.

"Fifty dollars," said he; "how much will that be apiece. Thirteen into fifty; can any of you fellers cipher that up in your heads?"

"Three and eleven thirteenths dollars each," said William Bright, who pulled the next oar forward of Tim. "Three dollars and eighty-five cents—isn't it?'

"Eighty-four and a fraction," replied Fred, with schoolboy accuracy.

"A feller could have a good time on that, I'll bet," ejaculated Tim.

"And many a poor man would like it to buy bread for his family," added Frank. "But there is the Butterfly!"

Tim Bunker dropped his oar at this announcement, and was on the point of rising to get a better view of the Zephyr's rival, when the handle of William Bright's oar gave him a smart rap in the back.

"Mind out!" said Tim. "Don't you know any better than to hit a feller in that way?"

"Cease — rowing!" called Frank, as he saw Tim's fist involuntarily double up, and his eye flash with anger.

"It was your fault, Tim, and you must not blame him," added the coxswain, mildly, but firmly.

"My fault!" and Tim added an expression which I cannot put upon my page.

"Such language as that is contrary to the constitution," continued Frank. "You stopped rowing without orders."

"What if I did!"

"You should not have done so. No member can do, or cease to do, without orders; that's our discipline."

Tim cooled off in a moment, made a surly apology for his rudeness, and the Zephyr continued on her course.

CHAPTER IV.

THE FRATERNAL HUG.

THE incident which had just occurred gave Frank considerable uneasiness   Tim was naturally quarrelsome, and his former mode of life had done nothing to improve his disposition.   He had never been taught that self-restraint is necessary to preserve social harmony.   If any thing did not suit him, he was not disposed to argue the matter in a conciliatory manner, but to right his wrongs, whether real or imaginary, by physical force.   In this manner he had obtained his reputation as a " good fighter."

Frank began to fear that Tim had come into the club without a proper understanding of its duties and requirements.   Though he had, with an ill grace, apologized for his conduct, he seemed to feel no compunction on account of it; but, on the contrary, he every moment grew more overbearing and insolent

He could not speak to his companions in a gentlemanly manner, as they had been accustomed to be
addressed. He was coarse, rude, and vulgar; and
the members, who had received him among them in
the best spirit possible, began to feel some repug-
nance towards him.

But what could be expected of him in so short a
time? They had no reason to believe that a boy
who had always been a desperado would suddenly
become a gentle and kind-hearted person. His nature wanted refining, and such a work could not be
done in a moment. These reflections came to
Frank's relief, when he had become well nigh discouraged at the idea of reforming Tim — discouraged
more by thinking of the vast chasm that yawned between what he was and what he ought to be. Like
the pendulum in the story, he was crowding the
work of months and years into a single instant. A
little sober thought in the proper direction set him
right.

The Butterfly was darting out of " Weston Bay "
as they approached.

" Cease — rowing ! " said Frank. " Now, my lads,

let us give them three rousing cheers. **All up!**
One ! "

" Hurrah !"

" Two."

" Hurrah !"

"Three."

" Hurrah !"

And then the Zephyrs clapped their hands, **long**
and loudly, and this was the greeting which the **old**
club gave to the new one. The compliment was
heartily returned by the Butterfly, and then the
cheers were repeated again and again. Every member seemed to glow with kindly feeling towards the
others. Even Tim Bunker for the time laid aside
his morose look, and joined in the expression of good
will with as much zeal as his companions.

" Now man your oars, Zephyrs," said Frank.

" What ye going to do now ? " asked Tim, as he
grasped his oar with the others.

" You shall know in due time," replied the coxswain.

Here was another thing which Tim had yet, to
learn — not to ask questions of the **commander.** It

5

was a part of the discipline of the club to obey
without stopping to argue the point.   Captain Sedley himself had suggested this idea, and it had been
thoroughly carried out on board the Zephyr.   It was
an established principle that " the coxswain knew
what he was about," and that he alone was responsible for the guidance and the safety of the boat.

Tim did not seem to fancy this kind of discipline.
He evidently felt that he had been born to command,
and not to obey.   But the consciousness that he was
in the minority induced him to yield whatever convictions he might have had of his own superiority to
the will of the " powers that be," and he followed
the example of the others.

"Ready — pull!" continued Frank.

He and Tony had arranged a little system of
" fleet manœuvres," to be carried out when the two
boats met.

To the surprise of all on board, — for they were
not " posted up" in regard to these tactics, —Frank
put the Zephyr about.

" Cease — rowing!" said he, when the boat was
headed in the opposite direction.

To the further surprise of the Zephyrs, they discovered that the Butterfly had executed a similar manœuvre, and that the two boats lay at the distance
of nearly a quarter of a mile apart, the bow of one
pointing directly east, and the other directly west.

"Ready to back her!" said Frank, and the boys
all pulled their oar handles close to their breasts,
ready at the word to take the reverse stroke.

"Back her!"

The Butterfly did the same thing exactly, and the
two boats rapidly approached each other, stern first
Tony had certainly made the most of the time which
had been allotted to him for drilling his crew, and
they worked together almost as well as the Zephyrs,
who were a little embarrassed at each new movement
by the awkwardness of Tim Bunker.

"Steady — slow," continued Frank, as the two
boats came nearer together. "That will do; cease
—rowing. Ready — up!" and the twelve oars
gleamed in the sunshine.

The sterns of the two boats came together, and
Frank threw Tony a line, which the latter made fast.

"Ready — down!" said Tony and Frank, almost

in the same breath ; and the oars were deposited in
their places on the thwarts.

The two clubs were facing each other as they sat
n their seats, with the respective coxswains standing
in the stern sheets.

" Mr. Coxswain of the Butterfly," said Frank, as
he removed his hat, and gracefully bowed to Tony,
" in behalf of the members of the Zephyr Boat
Club, of which you were so long a cnerished member, I welcome you and your club, and the beautiful craft in which you sail, to these waters. May
the Zephyr and the Butterfly cruise together in
entire harmony ; may no hard words or hard thoughts
be called forth by either, but may all be peace and
good will."

This little speech was received with a burst of applause by Tony's club, and the boats interchanged
volleys of cheers.

" Mr. Coxswain of the Zephyr," Tony began, in
reply to his friend's speech, " I am much obliged to
you and your companions for the kind words you
have spoken for yourself and for them. I am sure
there will never be any hard feelings between us, and

I assure you if any fellow in our club attempts to make a row, we will turn him out. Won't we, fellows?"

"Ay, ay! That we will," replied the club, with one voice.

"If we get beaten in a race, we will bear our defeat like men. Won't we, boys?"

That we will."

Tony wound up by saying he was not much at making speeches, but he was ready to do every thing he could to make things go off right and pleasantly

Three cheers more were given on each side, and the crews were ordered into their seats.

"Starboard oars, ready — up!" said Frank.

"Larboard oars, ready — up!" said Tony.

"Ready — down!" was then given by one, and repeated by the other. And then, "Ready — pull!' followed, in like manner.

My reader will readily perceive that the effect of this manœuvre was to turn the boats round in opposite directions, so that they came alongside of each other, after a few strokes of the oars.

The painter of the Butterfly was thrown on board

the Zephyr, and made fast to the bow ring. The boys were now all brought together, and the discipline of the clubs was relaxed so as to permit the members to enjoy a few moments of social recreation.

The Butterfly, as we have said in the introduction, was of the same size and model as the Zephyr, and, except that the former was painted in gayer colors, to represent the gaudy tints of the butterfly, the two boats were exact counterparts of each other.

Her crew had already procured their uniform, and wore it on the present occasion. It was a pair of white pants, made "sailor fashion," with a short red frock, and a patent-leather belt. These garments, owing to the coldness of the weather, were worn over their usual clothes. The hat was a tarpauling, with the name of the club in gilt letters on the front, and upon the left breast of the frock was a butterfly, worked in colors.

The Butterfly, like her rival, carried an American flag at the stern, and a blue silk fly, with the letter "B" or it, at the bow.

"This is glorious, isn't it, Frank?" said Tony, as he took his friend's hand and warmly pressed it.

"First rate! There is fun before us this season; and if nothing happens to mar the harmony which now prevails, we shall enjoy ourselves even more than we did last summer."

"Nothing can happen — can there?" replied Tony, glancing involuntarily at Tim Bunker, who seemed to be so amazed at the good will that prevailed around him as to be incapable of saying any thing.

"I hope not; but, Tony, what about the race? Has your club voted on the question of the prize?"

"Yes."

"What did you do?"

"What have you done, Frank?" asked Tony. There was not the slightest doubt as to his Yankee paternity.

"We voted to accept the offer."

"So did we, though our members were so afraid of doing something wrong, that George had to come into the meeting and argue the question with them. We accepted the offer on condition that you did so."

"Then it is all arranged."

"Yes, except the time."

"We shall leave that all to you."

" We are ready now," replied Tony, with a smile.

" Name the day, then."

" Next Wednesday afternoon."

" Very well."

" Who shall be the judges? We have chosen your father for one."

" And we shall choose Uncle Ben for another."

" Let us choose the other together."

" Agreed."

The two clubs were then called to order, and Frank, at Tony's request, stated the business to them.

" Please to nominate," said he.

" Mr. Hyde, the schoolmaster," exclaimed a dozen voices.

It was a unanimous vote, and the judges were all elected.

" Now, Tony, let us have some fun."

" We will try our fleet tactics a little more, if you like."

" So I say."

" We will go down the lake with the ' fraternal hug.' "

" The what ! " exclaimed Charles Hardy.

" We call our present position the 'fraternal hug.' "

" Hurrah for the fraternal hug ! " shouted Charles, and all the boys laughed heartily.

" Nothing bearish about it, I hope," added Fred Harper.

" We have no bears," replied Frank, as he ordered out his starboard oars.

Tony in like manner got out his larboard oars.

" Now, Frank," said he, " as you are a veteran in the service, you shall be commodore, and command the allied squadron."

A burst of laughter greeted this sally ; but Frank was too modest to accept this double command, and would only do so when a vote had been passed, making him " commodore."

Fenders — a couple of cushions, which Frank, in anticipation of this manœuvre, had provided — were placed between the two boats to keep them from injuring each other, and the order was given to pull. As but six oars were pulled in each boat, their progress was not very rapid. No one, however, seemed to care for that. The joining of the two boats in the "fraternal hug" was emblematic of the union that subsisted in the hearts of their crews, and all the members of each club seemed better satisfied with this symbolical expression of their feelings than though they had won a victory over the other.

When they came abreast of the Zephyr's boat house, they discovered that Uncle Ben was on board the Sylph, which lay moored at a short distance from the shore.

Bang! went the cannon which the veteran had again rigged on the bow of the sail boat.

And as they passed down the lake, Uncle Ben blazed away in honor of the fraternal hug between the two clubs.

CHAPTER V.

UP THE RIVER.

AT the end of the lake the boats separated, after giving each other three hearty cheers.

" Where are you going now? " asked Tim Bunker.

" We will go up the lake again."

" Suppose we try a race? " suggested Fred Harper.

" There will be no harm in it, I suppose," replied Frank, glancing at the Butterfly.

" Zephyr, ahoy! " shouted Tony. " We will pull up together, if you like."

" Agreed."

The two boats were then drawn up alongside of each other, ready to start when the word should be given.

" Say when you are ready," shouted Tony.

The rowers in each boat were all ready to take the first stroke.

"Ready — pull!" said Frank; and the crews bent to the work.

"Now give it to 'em!" shouted Tim Bunker, as he struck out with his oar.

' Steady, Tim," said Frank. "Be very careful, or you will lose the stroke."

"No, I won't. Put 'em through by daylight!" And Tim, without paying much attention to the swaying of the coxswain's body, by which his stroke should have been regulated, redoubled his exertions. He was very much excited, and the next moment the handle of his oar hit the boy in front of him in the back. Then the boy behind hit him, and a scene of confusion immediately ensued. Of course no boy could pull his stroke except in unison with the others; so the whole were compelled to cease rowing.

"We have lost it," said Frank, good naturedly.

The boys, seeing how useless it was to attempt to row in the midst of such confusion, were obliged to wait till order had been restored.

"No, we hain't; pull away!" replied Tim, as he seized his oar, and began to row with all his might

" Cease rowing ! " said Frank.

" Catch your oars, you sleepies, or they will get in first ! " exclaimed Tim, who continued to struggle with his oar in defiance of the order.

He had already pulled the boat half round.

" I guess the fifty dollars won't come to this crew," added Tim, contemptuously.

" It certainly will not, if you don't obey orders better than that," replied Frank.

" I don't want to have the club beat so easy as that."

" But it is all your fault, Tim."

" You lie ! "

" What ! what ! " exclaimed Frank. " We cannot have such language as that. If you don't conform to the constitution you have signed, you shall be put on shore at the nearest land."

" Well, I ain't a going to have it laid to me, when I hain't done nothing. Didn't I pull with all my might and main ? and if the other fellers had done so too, we should been ahead of 'em afore this time," answered Tim, somewhat tamed by the threat of the coxswain.

"We will not talk about that until you say whether you intend to conform to the rules of the club, or not," added Frank, firmly.

"Of course I do."

Tim was still gruff in his tones; but it was evident that he wanted to conform to the rules, and that his obstinacy was still struggling for expression.

"You must not tell the coxswain, or any other member, that he lies, Tim," continued Frank.

"That was a slip of the tongue."

The Bunker tried to laugh it off, and declared that he was so used to that form of expression he could not leave it off at once. This was regarded as a great concession by all.

"Very well; if you will promise to do your best to obey the rules, we will say no more about it."

"Of course I will," replied Tim, with a laugh, which was equivalent to saying, "If any of you think I am yielding too much, why, I am only joking."

"Now, Tim, that point being settled, I repeat that our mishap was caused by you, though we don't blame you for it. You meant to do your best, but you didn't go to work in the right way."

" What's the reason I didn't ? "

" You broke up the stroke."

" The fellers ought to have pulled faster, then, so as to keep up with me ; if they had, we should have done well enough."

" That is not the way.   The coxswain is to judge how fast you may pull with safety."

" Just as you like.   All I wanted was to win the race."

" I understand you ; but we can do nothing if the discipline of the club is not observed."

" I didn't know about that."

" Let us understand one another for the future. You must regulate your stroke by the motion of my body.   You are to see nothing but me ; and whatever happens, you must obey orders."

" Let's try it again.   I will do as you say," replied Tim, with a great deal more gentleness than he had before shown.

"Ready — pull ! " said Frank.   And away darted the Zephyr up the lake.

Tim pulled very steadily now, and showed a disposition to do as the others did, and to obey orders

Frank was pleased with the result of the conference, and began to entertain strong hopes of the ultimate reformation of the Bunker.

But the race was lost; the Butterfly was almost at the head of the lake.

"There's a chance for the Butterflies to crow over us," said Tim, after a silence of several moments.

"There is to be no crowing. If we had beaten them, I should not have permitted a word to be spoken that would create a hard feeling in the minds of any of them," replied Frank. "And I know that Tony is exactly of my mind."

"It is no great credit to them to have beaten us under these circumstances," added Fred.

"Each club must be responsible for its own discipline. No excuses are to be pleaded. Good order and good regulations will prevent such accidents as just befell us."

"That is what discipline is for," said William Bright.

"Exactly so. Don't you remember what Mr. Hyde told me when I tried to excuse myself for not having my sums done with the plea that I had ας pencil ?" asked Charles Hardy. "He said it waa us much a part of our duty to be ready for our work us it was to do it after we were ready."

"That's good logic," put in Fred. "If the engine companies did not keep their machines in good working order, of course they would render no service at the fire. You remember Smith's factory was burnt because 'No. 2's' suction hose leaked, and the 'tub' couldn't be worked."

"That's it; in time of peace prepare for war."

"Where s the Butterfly now?" asked Tim, who did not feel much interest in this exposition of duty.

"She is headed up to Rippleton River," replied Frank. "I hope she does not mean to venture among the rocks."

Rippleton River was a stream which emptied into the lake at its eastern extremity. Properly speaking, Wood Lake was only a widening of this river, though the stream was very narrow, and discharged itself into the lake amid immense masses of rock.

The mouth of this river was so obstructed by these rocks, that Captain Sedley had forbidden the boys ever to venture upon its waters; though, with

occasional difficulties in the navigation, it was deep
enough and wide enough to admit the passage of
the boat for several miles.   A wooden bridge crossed
the stream a little way above the lake — an old, de-
cayed affair which had frequently been complained
of as unsafe.

" Tony knows the place very well," said Charles
" He will not be rash."

" But there he goes right in amongst the rocks,
and the Butterflies are pulling with all their might.
He is crazy," added Frank, his countenance exhibiting the depth of his anxiety.

" Let Tony alone ; he knows what he is about,"
responded Fred.

" Heavens ! " exclaimed Frank, suddenly, as he
rose in his place.   " There has been an accident at
the bridge !   I see a horse and chaise in the river."

Tim dropped his oar, and was turning round to
get a view of the object, when Frank checked him
So strict was the discipline of the club, that, notwithstanding the excitement which the coxswain's
announcement tended to create, not another boy
ceased rowing, or even missed his stroke.

"Keep your seat," said Frank to Tim. "Take your oar."

"I want to see what's going on," replied Tim.

"Keep your seat," repeated Frank, authoritatively.

Tim concluded to obey; and without a word resumed his place, and commenced pulling again.

"Tony is after them; if you obey orders we may get there in' season to render some assistance," continued Frank. "Don't balk us now, Tim."

"I won't, Frank; I will obey all your orders. I didn't think when I got up," replied Tim, with earnestness, and withal in such a tone that Frank's hopes ran high.

"Will you cross the rocks, Frank?" asked Charles Hardy.

"Certainly."

"But you know your father told us never to go into the river."

"Circumstances alter cases."

"But it will be disobedience under any circumstances."

"We won't argue the point now," answered the

bold coxswain, quickening the movements of his body till the crew pulled with their utmost strength and speed, and the Zephyr flew like a rocket over the water.

"I don't like to go, Frank, and though I will obey orders, I now protest against this act of disobedience," replied Charles, who was sure this time that Captain Sedley would commend and approve his inflexible love of obedience.

"Pull steady, and mind your stroke," added Frank, whose eye was fixed upon the chaise in the water.

"We may strike upon the rocks and be dashed to pieces," suggested Charles.

"If you are afraid ——"

"O, no! I'm not afraid; I was thinking of the boat."

"If it is dashed to pieces in a good cause, let it be so."

"Good!" ejaculated Fred Harper. "That's the talk for me!"

"The water in the lake is very high, and I know exactly where the rocks lie. Keep steady; I will put you through in safety."

"Where is the Butterfly now, Frank?" asked William Bright.

"Wait a minute. — There she goes! Hurrah! she has passed the reefs safely. They pull like heroes. There! Up go ncr oars — they are inboard. There are a man and a woman in the water, struggling for life. The man is trying to save the woman. The chaise seems to hang upon a rock, and the horse is kicking and plunging to clear himself, Steady — pull steady."

"Tony will save them all," said Fred.

"Hurrah! there he goes overboard, with half a dozen of his fellows after him! There are six left in the boat, and they are working her along towards the man and woman. They have them — they are safe. Now they pull the lady in — hah — all right! 1 was afraid they would upset the boat. They have got her in, and the man is holding on at the stern. Tony has got a rope round the horse's neck, and the fellows are clearing him from the chaise."

The Zephyr was now approaching the dangerous rocks, and Frank was obliged to turn his attention to the steering of the boat through the perilous passage.

"Steady," said he, "and pull strong. All right; we are through. We are too late to do any thing. They have landed the man and woman, and now they are towing the horse ashore. Tony's a glorious fellow ! He is worth his weight in solid gold ! "

" Can't we save the chaise ? " asked Tim Bunker.

" We can try."

" Hurrah for the chaise then ! "

" Bowman, get the long painter ahead," continued Frank.

" Ay, ay."

The coxswain of the Zephyr steered her towards the vehicle, which still hung to the rock, and, by a skilful manœuvre, contrived to make fast the line to one of the shafts of the chaise.

" Ready — pull ! " said Frank, as he passed the line over one of the thwarts.

The crew pulled with a will, and the jerk disengaged the chaise, and they succeeded in hauling it safely to the shore, and placing it high and dry upon the rocks.

CHAPTER VI.

HURRAH FOR TONY!

Tony and his six companions, who had been with him in the river, stood on the rocks shivering with cold, when the Zephyr's crew landed. The rest of her boys had been sent to conduct the lady and gentleman to the nearest house, and render them such assistance as they might require.

"You are a brave fellow, Tony!" said Frank, warmly, as he grasped the wet hand of his friend.

"I am very wet and cold, whatever else I may be," replied Tony, trying to laugh, while his teeth chattered so that he could hardly speak.

"You had better go home; you will catch cold," continued Frank.

"We must wait for the fellows."

"No, you shall take six of the Zephyr's crew, and pull home as fast as you can, and we will wait for the rest."

"We can do no more good here ; so we may as well go. Thank you for your offer, Frank, and I will accept it. If you like I will take Fred Harper to steer down, for I should like to pull an oar myself to warm up with."

"Certainly ;" and Frank detailed six of his club, including Fred, who seated themselves in the Butterfly.

"I don't know about those rocks, Tony," said Fred, as he grasped the tiller ropes.

"The water is so high, that there is no danger. I will have an eye to the passage when we get to it," replied Tony, as he took his old place at the bow oar.

The Butterfly pushed off, and in a few moments after passed the dangerous rocks in safety. Her crew pulled with energy, and it is quite likely that they got warm before they reached the boat house.

It was some time before the rest of the Butterfly's crew returned to the rocks where they had landed.

"Where's Tony ?" asked one of them, a boy of fourteen, but so small in stature that his companions had nicknamed him "Little Paul," of whom we shall have more to say by and by.

"They have gone home; we sent six of our fellows with them. They were too wet and cold to stay here," replied Frank. "You can return in our boat."

"The gentleman wants to see Tony very much."

"Who is he?"

"His name is Walker; it would do your heart good to hear him speak of Tony."

"I dare say; but Tony is worthy of all the praise that can be bestowed upon him. How is the lady?"

"She is nicely, and *she* thinks Tony is an angel. She declares that a dozen strong men could have done no more for them."

"She is right; **you** did all that could have been done by any persons. The Butterfly's first laurel is a glorious one, and I can congratulate you on the honors you have won."

"Thank you, Frank," said Little Paul, modestly. "I am sorry you were not with us to share the honors."

"We should have been, if it hadn't been for Tim Bunker," said Charles Hardy a little sourly.

7

Tim had gone with the Butterfly, or Charles would not have dared to make such a remark.

"And if you had had your way, we shouldn't have come when we did," added William Bright, smartly.

"What do you mean, Bill?"

"Didn't you protest against passing the rocks?"

"I did, because it was directly in opposition to Captain Sedley's orders."

"Never mind, fellows," interposed Frank; "for my part, I am glad the Butterfly had it all to herself. She has just come out, and it will be a feather in her cap."

"But we saved the chaise," said Charles.

"We pulled it ashore; it was safe enough where it was. The Butterfly saved the lives of the man, and woman, and the horse. They would have drowned, and all the glory consisted in saving them. Tony and his crew deserve all the credit, and I, for one, am happy to accord it to them."

"That's just like you, Frank!" exclaimed Little Paul. "I believe, if the two boats had changed places, you would have given us all the credit."

" You behaved nobly."

" Just as you would have done if you had been in Tony's place."

" We will talk that over some other time. We are ready to return when you are."

" I suppose there is nothing more to be done."

They were about to embark, when they discovered a party of men approaching the place, several of them carrying ropes and poles.

" Hold on!" shouted Farmer Leeds, to whose house the boys had conducted the lady and gentleman. " We want your boat to get the chaise out of the river with."

" It is out now," replied Little Paul.

The boys waited till the party reached the river. A clump of trees had prevented them from seeing the chaise till they had got almost to the shore; and, as Little Paul expressed it afterwards, " they looked surprised enough, to see it high and dry upon the rocks."

" I must say one thing, Mr. Leeds," began Mr. Walker; " and that is, you have smart boys in this vicinity."

" Toler'ble," replied the farmer, with a smile.

" They are men in noble deeds."

" This boating business turns the boys into men; and though, in my opinion, it would be just as well to set 'em to work in the cornfields, there is no denying that it brings 'em out, and makes 'em smart."

" My wife would certainly have been drowned without their help."

" I dare say."

" But where is the little fellow that commanded the boat?" asked Mr. Walker, scrutinizing the faces of the boys.

" He has gone home, sir; he was wet and cold."

" That is right; I am glad he has; I shall go and see him by and by. And these are the boys that brought the chaise ashore?"

" Yes, sir," replied Little Paul." This is Frank Sedley, the coxswain of the Zephyr.

" Well, Master Sedley, I am under great obliga-tions to you."

" Not at all to me, sir. Tony Weston saved you. We only pulled the chaise ashore.'

" But you shall not be forgotten. The other boat is gone, you say?"

" Yes, sir. Tony Weston is the coxswain of the Butterfly."

" And a noble fellow he is, too. He will be a great man one of these days. It did my heart good to see how cool and collected he was; how skilfully he managed the boat, when it came down upon us like a race horse. He gave off his orders like a hero, and they were obeyed with a promptness and precision that would have been creditable to the crew of a man of war, after a three years' cruise. And then, when he ordered six of the boys to stay in the boat, and the rest to follow him into the water, it was really heroic. Over he went, with his crew after him, as though they had been so many ducks. And in the water, they worked with as much coolness and courage as though it had been their native element. I would give half my fortune to be the father of such a son."

" I would give all of mine," added Farmer Leeds. " You don't know half his worth yet But there is nothing for us to do here; the men shall haul your chaise up to the house, and as we walk along I will tell you about Tony."

"Master Sedley, I shall see you again to-day or to-morrow. Tell Tony how highly I value his noble service, and tell him I shall call upon him this evening," said Mr. Walker, as he went away with Farmer Leeds.

"My father would be very happy to have you stop at his house while you remain in Rippleton," continued Frank, who was not sure that the farm house would accommodate him.

"As to that," interposed Farmer Leeds, "I can't offer you so grand a house as Captain Sedley's, but such as it is, you are welcome to it."

"Thank you, Master Sedley, for your hospitable invitation; but I think I will remain with my good friend here." And he departed with the farmer.

"All aboard!" said Frank, and the boys tumbled into the boat, and grasped their oars.

The Zephyr pushed off, and her cheerful crew pulled merrily down the river. Frank was conscious that the organization of the boat clubs had been the means of accomplishing the good work which the crew of the Butterfly had just achieved. He was aware that some of the people in the vicinity had cherished strong objections to the clubs, and that Tony had had considerable difficulty in persuading the parents of his crew to allow their sons to join. The adventure at the bridge, he thought, would have a tendency to reconcile them, and to elevate and dignify boating. At any rate a good deed had been done, and the parents of those who had taken part in it could not but be proud of the laurels their sons had earned.

The Zephyr, under Frank's skilful pilotage, passed the rocks in safety, though, as they darted through the narrow channel, he could see their sharp edges only a little way below the surface of the clear water.

They had scarcely entered the open lake before they perceived the Sylph, under full sail with a smashing breeze, close aboard of them.

" Frank ." shouted Captain Sedley, who was at the helm, while Uncle Ben was gazing at them with a very sorrowful face from the half deck.

" Ay, ay, sir!" replied Frank, as he laid the Zephyr's course towards the sail boat.

Though his father had only spoken his name, there was something in the tone which could not be misapprehended; but it did not occur to him, he was so engaged in thinking of the incidents at the bridge, that he had disobeyed his father's command in passing into the river.

As the Zephyr approached, the Sylph luffed, and came up into the wind, to wait for her. Frank brought his boat round under the stern of the sail boat, and "lay to" an oar's length from her.

"Frank," said his father, sternly, "I am surprised that you should venture among those rocks, when I have expressly forbidden you ever to go into the river."

"But, father, there was ——"

"How could you do such a thing, after I had so carefully warned you — so positively interdicted it? Suppose your boat had been dashed in pieces," continued Captain Sedley, who, though deeply grieved at his son's apparent disobedience, was too indignant to hear an excuse; for such he supposed Frank was about to offer — one of those silly, frivolous excuses which boys sometimes seize upon to palliate their misconduct.

"I protested against it!" said Charles Hardy rising from his seat.

"Shut up!" exclaimed Little Paul, his cheek glowing with indignation, as he pulled Charles back into his seat.

"I went to save life, father," replied Frank, almost choked by his emotions, a flood of tears springing in his eyes and well nigh blinding him.

"To save life!" said Captain Sedley, touched by the reply, and far more by Frank's emotion.

He saw that he had spoken too quick — that his son had not passed the rocks without a good and sufficient reason.

"Yes, sir," replied Frank, struggling to master his feelings; and then he related all that had occurred at the bridge; how Tony had saved the lady and gentleman, and the horse; and how his crew had pulled the chaise ashore.

"You did right, Frank; forgive my hasty words," said Captain Sedley, with deep feeling.

"Good, my hearty!" exclaimed Uncle Ben, clapping his hands.

A heavy load had been removed from the mind of the veteran, who had almost come to believe that Frank *could* do no wrong.

" 'Tony's a hero; and shiver my timbers, if he oughtn't to be president of the United States, when he's old enough," exclaimed Uncle Ben.

" He is a brave fellow. You have done well, both of you. However strict our orders are, no person should be a machine. Orders should be obeyed with judgment," continued Captain Sedley.

" That's a fact. I could tell a yarn about that," added Uncle Ben. " When I was in the old Varsayles, bound round the Horn —— "

" Another time we will hear your yarn, Ben," interposed Captain Sedley. " We will go over and see Tony now, and congratulate him on the honors the Butterfly has won. Haul in the gib sheet, Ben."

" Ready — pull ! " said Frank.

" Who protested now, Master Charles Hardy ? " asked Little Paul, as he goodnaturedly punched the forward youth in the ribs.

" Circumstances alter cases," replied Charles, sagely, as he bent on his oar."

" Fact ! but they altered them when the deed was done, not now, when you have found out that it was all right."

CHAPTER VII.

COMMODORE FRANK SEDLEY

FOR a few days all Rippleton rang with the praises of Tony and his companions. All the particulars of the affair at the bridge had been given in the Rippleton Mercury, and the editor was profuse in his commendations of the skill and courage of the Butterfly Boat Club; and he did not withhold from the Zephyr the credit which was justly due. Tony was a hero, and his fame extended for many miles around.

Mr. Walker and his lady, who had been rescued from the river, visited Captain Sedley and the Weston family the next day. I need not tell my young readers how earnest he was in the expression of his admiration and gratitude. He was a wealthy merchant, and resided in a neighboring town. Being as warm hearted and generous as he was just and discriminating, it was quite natural that he should give his feelings expression in some substantial token of his gratitude.

Before he left Rippleton, a check for five hundred dollars was placed in the hands of George Weston, with directions to give four hundred of it to the Butterfly, and one hundred to the Zephyr. In the division of the Butterfly's share, Mr. Walker desired that one hundred dollars should be given to Tony, and twenty-five dollars apiece to the crew; consenting, however, to let the whole sum be common property if the club desired.

This liberality was certainly munificent, princely; but Mr. Walker's wealth was quite sufficient to enable him to gratify his generous impulses. Tony said he felt a little "ticklish" about taking it, at first; but George assured him that Mr. Walker would feel hurt if he did not, and he concluded to accept it.

"But what shall we do with it, George?" asked the young hero, who was not a little embarrassed by the possession of so much money.

"That is for you to decide."

8

" What *can* we do with it ? "

" It will buy heaps of candy," suggested George with a smile.

" Candy !" said Tony, contemptuously.

" You can make a fund of it if you like."

" What for ? "

" For any purpose you may wish.   By and by you may want money for something."

" What shall we do with it ? "

" Put it in the Savings Bank."

" But the next thing is, shall we divide it ? or let it remain as the property of the club?   I suppose the fellows will all do just as I do."

" Perhaps the money would do the parents of some of them a great deal of good."

" I think very likely ; we will let them vote upon it.   Here comes Frank.   I wonder what they are going to do with theirs."

" How do you do, Tony?   I have come over to talk with you about the race.   Next Wednesday is the day, you know."

" I had forgotten all about the race in the excitement of the bridge affair."

"I don't wonder."

"What are you going to do with your money, Frank?" asked Tony. "Your club met last evening, I believe."

"We voted to buy some philosophical apparatus with it."

"Good! Did Tim Bunker vote for that?"

"He didn't vote at all. He wanted the money divided; but the vote was unanimous for spending it as I said. By the way, Mr. Walker was liberal — wasn't he?"

"Princely. He ought to have given you more and us less, though."

"No; he did perfectly right. We did not deserve even what we got."

"Just like you! But come into the club room — Butterfly Hall — and we will fix things for the race."

Frank and Tony discussed the details of the race, and at the end of an hour every thing was arranged to the satisfaction of both. There was no difference of opinion except as to the length of the race. Tony thought that twice up and down the lake, making an eight-mile race, would be best; but Frank felt sure that it was too long, and that it would tire the boys too much. So it was finally agreed that they should pull only once up and down, making about four miles.

As the Butterfly club were to meet that evening, Frank departed earlier than he otherwise would have done, so as not to be considered an intruder.

Tony's club were in high spirits that evening. The praise bestowed upon them had created a strong feeling of self-reliance in their minds. Their discipline had passed through a severe ordeal, and it was pronounced perfectly satisfactory by all concerned. They had done hard work, and done it well. Their success was the result of their excellent discipline. It would have been in vain that they had as good a commander as Tony, if promptness and obedience had been wanting.

" Now, boys," said Tony, when he had called the meeting to order, " we have arranged all the details of the race, and if you like, I will tell you about it."

" Tell us," said several.

The chairman proceeded to give them the substance of his conversation with the coxswain of the Zephyr ; and the rules they had adopted were of course agreed to by all present.

The Butterfly boys, elated with the results of the bridge affair, were confident that they should win the race. Tony, however, was not so sanguine. He knew, better than they, how skilful Frank was ; and, if the Zephyr had not labored under the disadvantage of having a new member, he would have been sure of being beaten.

"There is another subject which comes up for consideration to-night — I mean the gift of Mr. Walker. He has left it so that it may be divided among us, or held and used as common property," continued Tony.

The boys looked at each other, as if to pry into the thoughts of their neighbors. There was a long silence, and it was in vain that Tony called for the opinions of the members ; they did not seem to have any opinions on the subject.

"We will do just as you say, Mr. Chairman," said Little Paul.

"So we will," added Henry Brown.

8 *

" I sl all not say," replied Tony.   " It is a mattoɪ
foɪ you to decide.   George says wc can put it in the
Savings Bank, if we don't divide it, and keep it till
we find a use for it.   Perhaps, though, some of your
parents may want it.   If they do, we had· better
givᴇ each his share."

"Let us put it in the Savings Bank," said Dick
Chester.

But Henry Brown looked at Little Paul, whose
father was a very poor man, and had not been able
to work for several months.

" Perhaps we had better divide it," suggested he.

" If you agree to divide it, each member shall
have a thirteenth part of the whole four hundred
dollars," added Tony.

" That wouldn't be right," replied Little Paul.
' He gave a hundred to you ; and certainly you are
better entitled to a hundred than we are to a penny
apiece."

" I will not take more than my share."

" We will only take what Mr. Walker awardᴉd
ns," said Henry.

" That we won't," added several members.

"No!" shouted the whole club.

" But you *shall*, my lads," said Tony, stoutly " George and I have agreed to that."

" But the commander of the ship ought to have a bigger share than the crew; besides, what could we have done without you?" argued Little Paul.

" And what could I have done without you?"

"It was your skill and courage, as the Mercury says, which did the business."

" It was your prompt obedience that crowned our labors with success. I tell you, boys, it is just as broad as it is long. The money shall be equally divided."

" Then we won't divide it," said Henry Brown.

" Very well; I will agree to that. We shall be equal owners then," replied Tony, with a smile of triumph; for in either case his point was gained.

" But what shall we do with it? Four hundred dollars is a heap of money. What's the use of saving it up without having some idea of what we mean to do with it? "

" We can put it to a dozen uses."

" What, for instance ? "

"Why, enlarging our library; buying an appara·
tas, as the Zephyrs are going to do ; giving it to the
poor," replied Tony. "But I was thinking of something before the meeting."

The boys all looked at the chairman with inquir-
ing glances.

"Out with it," said several of them.

"There are lots of fellows round here who would
like to get into a boat club."

"More than twenty," added Little Paul. '

"We have money enough to buy another boat."

"Hurrah!" exclaimed several of the members,
jumping out of their chairs in the excitement of the
moment. "Let us buy another boat!"

"What shall we call her?" added Dick Chester.

Several of the boys began to exercise their minds
on this important question, without devoting any
more attention to the propriety or the practicability
of procuring another boat. That question was re
garded as already settled.

"Ay, what shall we call her?" repeated Joseph
Hooper.

"What do you say to the 'Lily?'"

"The 'Water Sprite?'"

"The 'Go-ahead?'"

"Name her after Mr. Walker."

"No; after Tony Weston."

"You are counting the chickens before they are hatched," added Tony, laughing heartily.

"The — the — the 'Red Rover,'" said Joseph Hooper.

"That's too piratical," replied Little Paul.

"I wouldn't say any thing about the name at present," suggested Tony.

"Wouldn't it be fine, though, to have three boats on the lake?" exclaimed Henry.

"Glorious! A race with three boats!"

"Who would be coxswain of the new boat?"

"Fred Harper," said Little Paul. "The fellows say he is almost as good as Frank Sedley."

"If we had another boat we should want a commodore," continued Tony. "And I was thinking, if we got another, that Frank would be the commodore, and command the fleet. Then there would be a coxswain to each boat besides."

"That would be first rate."

" Let us have the other boat."

" Hurrah ! so I say."

" I suppose we could buy two six-oar boats for our money," added Tony.

" And have four in the fleet ? "

" Perhaps three four-oar boats."

" Five boats in the fleet !   That would be a glori-ous squadron ! "

The boys could hardly repress the delight which these air castles excited, and several of them kept jumping up and down, they were so nervous and so elated.

" Come, Tony, let us settle the business, and order the boats at once," said Dick Chester.

" We had better think a while of it.   Something else may turn up which will suit us even better than the fleet.   Of course we must consult Captain Sedley and George before we do any thing," replied Tony.

" They will be willing."

" Perhaps they will, and perhaps they won't."

" I know they will," said Dick.

" We will consult them, at any rate.   It is necessary to take a vote concerning the division of the money."

Of course the club voted not to divide; and it was decided that the money should remain in the hands of George Weston until the fleet question should be settled.

"Now, boys," said Tony, "next Monday is town meeting day, and school don't keep. We will meet at nine o'clock and practise for the race, which comes off on Wednesday afternoon, at three o'clock. Let every fellow be on hand in season."

The club adjourned, and the boys went off in little parties, discussing the exciting topic of a fleet of five boats, under the command of Commodore Frank Sedley.

CHAPTER VIII.

THE RACE.

THE day appointed for the race between the Zephyr and the Butterfly had arrived, and the large number of people congregated on the shores of Wood Lake testified to the interest which was felt in the event. Probably the exciting incident at the bridge, which had been published in the newspaper, imparted a greater degree of interest to the race than it would otherwise have possessed. It was a beautiful afternoon, mild and pleasant for the season, which favored the attendance of the ladies, and the lake was lined with a row of cheerful faces.

" All aboard ! " said Frank, as he dissolved a meeting of the Zephyrs, which he had called in order to impart whatever hints he had been able to obtain from his father and others in regard to their conduct.

Above all, he had counselled them, in case they

were beaten, to cherish no hard feelings towards
their rivals.   Not a shadow of envy or ill will was
to obscure the harmony of the occasion.   And if
they were so fortunate as to win the race, they were
to wear their honors with humility ; and most especially, they were not to utter a word which could
create a hard feeling in the minds of their competi-
tors.   Whatever the result, there was to be the same
kindness in the heart, and the same gentlemanly deportment in the manners, which had thus far charac-
terized the intercourse of the two clubs.

" All aboard ! "

The Zephyrs were more quiet and dignified in
their deportment than usual.   There was no loud
talk, no jesting ; even Fred Harper looked thoughtful
and serious.   Each member seemed to feel the respon-
sibility of winning the race, resting like a heavy
burden upon his shoulders.

The boat was hauled out into the lake, and once
more Frank cautioned them to keep cool and obey
orders.

" Don't look at the Butterfly after we get started,"
said he.   " You must permit me to keep watch of

9

her. Keep both eyes on me, and think only of
having your stroke perfectly accurate, perfectly in
time with the others. Now, remember, don't look
at the Butterfly; if you do, we shall lose the race.
It would distract your attention, and add to your
excitement. If she gets two or three lengths ahead
of us, as I think she will on the first mile, don't
mind it. Pull your best, and leave the rest with
me."

"Ay, ay!" replied several, quietly.

"Do you think we shall win, Frank?" asked
Charles, who had put the same question a dozen
times before.

"We must *think* that we shall," replied Frank,
with a smile. "Here comes the Butterfly. Now,
give her three cheers. One!"

"Hurrah!"

"Two!"

"Hurrah!"

"Three"

"Hurrah!"

This compliment was promptly returned by the
Butterfly, as she came alongside the Zephyr.

" Quarter of three, Frank," said Tony.

" Time we were moving then," replied Frank, as he ordered the oars out, and the boats started for the spot where the Sylph, the judges' boat, had taken position.

They pulled with a very slow stroke, and not only did the respective crews keep the most exact time, but each timed its stroke with the other. It was exhibition day with them, and they were not only to run the race, but to show off their skill to the best advantage. Hundreds of people, their fathers and their mothers, their sisters and their brothers, were observing them from the shore, and this fact inspired them to work with unusual care.

It was a very beautiful sight, those richly ornamented boats, their gay colors flashing in the bright sunshine, with their neatly uniformed crews, their silken flags floating to the breeze, and their light, graceful oars dipping with mechanical precision in the limpid waters. As they glided gently over the rippling waves, like phantoms, to the middle of the lake, a long and deafening shout from the shore saluted their ears. The white handkerchiefs of the ladies waved them a cheerful greeting, and the Rippleton Brass Band, which had volunteered for the occasion, struck up Hail Columbia.

"Cease — rowing!" said Frank, as he rose in his seat.

Tony followed his example, though this movement had not been laid down in the programme.

Frank then took the American flag which floated at the stern, and Tony did the same.

"All up!" said he. "Let us give them three cheers."

"Mind the coxswain of the Zephyr," added Tony, "and let them be all together and with a will."

"Hats off, and swing them as you cheer."

The cheers were given with all the vigor which stout lungs could impart, and the flags waved and the hats swung.

The salute was reiterated from the shore, and above the martial strains of the band rose the deafening hurrahs.

"Ready — pull!" and the boats resumed their slow and measured stroke, and the band changed the tune to the Canadian Boat Song.

When they reached the judges' boat, the two coxswains drew lots for the choice of "position," and the Butterfly obtained this advantage. The two boats then took their places, side by side, about two rods apart, ready to commence the race.

"Tony," said Frank, rising, "before we start I have a word to say. Whatever may be the result of the race, for myself and my crew, I pledge you there shall be no hard feeling among the Zephyrs."

"No, no, no!" added the club, earnestly.

"If you beat, it shall not impair our friendship; there shall be no envy, no ill will. Do you all say so, Zephyrs?"

"Ay, ay!"

The Butterflies clapped their hands vigorously, in token of their approbation of the pledge, and Tony promised the same thing for his club.

"Now we are ready," added Frank. "Keep perfectly cool, and mind all I have said. Ready!"

Uncle Ben stood in the bow of the Sylph, with a burning slow match in his hand, ready to discharge the cannon which was to be the signal for starting

9 *

It was a moment of intense excitement, not only to the crews of the boats, but to hundreds of spectators on the shore.

It was undeniably true that the Zephyrs, in spite of the warnings which Frank had given them, were very much excited, and various were the expedients which the boys used to calm their agitation, or at least to conceal it. But it was also true that the Buterflies were much more excited. Discipline and experience had not schooled them in the art of " being mere machines," and they found it much more difficult than the Zephyrs to subdue their troublesome emotions.

The eventful moment had come. The oarsmen were bent forward ready to strike the first stroke, and the coxswains were leaning back ready to time the movement. Captain Sedley was gazing intently at the dial of his "second indicator," prepared to give Uncle Ben the word to fire.

" Ready, Ben — fire ! "

Bang went the cannon.

" Pull ! " shouted Frank and Tony in the same breath.

Fortunately every oarsman in both boats hit the stroke exactly, and away leaped the gallant barks.

As Frank had deemed it probable, the Butterfly shot a length ahead of her rival after pulling a few strokes; but though the noise of the oars informed his crew of their relative positions, not an eye was turned from him, not a muscle yielded in the face of the dispiriting fact, and not a member quickened his stroke in order to retrieve the lost ground. Even Tim Bunker, who was supposed to have more feeling in regard to the race than the others, maintained an admirable self-possession. However much the hearts of the crew beat with agitation, they were outwardly as cool as though the Butterfly had been a mile behind them.

It is true, some of the Zephyrs, as they continued to gaze at Frank's calm and immovable features, wondered that he did not quicken the stroke; but no one for an instant lost confidence in him. "Frank knew what he was about." This was the sentiment that prevailed, and each member looked out for himself, leaving all the rest to him.

The Butterflies were quickening their stroke every

moment, and consequently were continuing to increase the distance between the two boats. Every
muscle was strained to its utmost tension. Every
particle of strength was laid out, until Tony, fearful
that some of the weaker ones might " make a slip,"
dared require no more of them. But they were
already more than two boats' lengths ahead of their
rival, and he had every thing to hope.

Still the Zephyr pulled that same steady stroke.
As yet she had made no extraordinary exertion. Her
crew were still fresh and vigorous, while those of her
rival, though she was every moment gaining upon
her, were taxing their strength to the utmost.

They rounded the stake boat, which had been
placed nearly opposite the mouth of Rippleton River,
and the Butterfly was full three lengths ahead. They
had begun upon the last two miles of the race.
Though the Zephyr still pursued her former tactics,
her rival was no longer able to gain upon her. The
latter had thus far done her best, and for the next
half mile the boats maintained the same relative positions.

Frank was still unmoved, and there was some

inward grumbling among his crew. An expression of deep anxiety had begun to supplant the look of hope and confidence they had worn, and some of them were provoked to a doubt whether Frank, in the generosity of his nature, was not intending to let Tony bear off the honors.

"Come, Frank, let her have, now!" said Tim, who could no longer restrain his impatience.

"Silence! Not a word!" said the self-possessed coxswain.

It was in the "order of the day" that no member should speak during the race; and none did, except Tim, and he could easily have been pardoned under the circumstances.

Not yet did Frank quicken the stroke of the Zephyr, though at the end of the next half mile she was only two boat lengths astern of her competitor, which had lost this distance by the exhaustion of her crew. They had pulled three miles with the expenditure of all their strength. They lacked the power of endurance, which could only be obtained by long practice. "It is the last pound that breaks the camel's back;" and it was so with them. With a little less exertion they might have preserved some portion of their vigor for the final struggle, which was yet to come.

They had begun upon the last mile. The crew of the Butterfly were as confident of winning the race as though the laurel of victory had already been awarded to them; and though their backs ached and their arms were nearly numb, a smile of triumph rested on their faces.

"Now for the tug of war," said Frank, in a low, subdued tone, loud enough to be heard by all his crew, but so gentle as not to create any of that dangerous excitement which is sometimes the ruin of the best laid plans.

As he spoke the motions of his body became a little quicker, and gradually increased in rapidity till the stroke was as quick as was consistent with perfect precision. The result of this greater expenditure of power was instantly observed, and at the end of the next quarter of a mile the boats were side by side again.

"They are beating us!" said Tony, in a whisper "Dip a little deeper — pull strong!"

The exciting moment of the race had come. The spectators on the shore gazed with breathless interest upon the spectacle, unable, though "Zephyr stock was up," to determine the result.

Not a muscle in Frank's face moved, and steadily and anxiously his crew watched and followed his movements.

"Steady!" said he, in his low, impressive tone, as he quickened a trifle more the stroke of the crew.

The Butterflies were "used up," incapable of making that vigorous effort which might have carried them in ahead of the Zephyr.

"A little deeper," continued Frank. "Now for it!"

As he spoke, with a sudden flash of energy he drove his oarsmen to their utmost speed and strength, and the Zephyr shot by the judges' boat full a length and a half ahead of the Butterfly.

"Cease — rowing!" said he. "Ready — up!"

The Butterfly came in scarcely an instant behind,

and her oars were poised in air, like those of her rival.

A long and animating shout rang along the shore, when the result of the race was apparent, and the band struck up "See the conquering hero comes."

CHAPTER IX.

LITTLE PAUL.

"You have won the race, Frank, and I congratulate you," said Tony Weston, as the Butterfly came alongside the Zephyr.

"Thank you, Tony; that is noble and generous," replied Frank.

"But it is the feeling in our club — isn't it, fellows?"

"Ay, ay, that it is!" shouted Little Paul. "Let us give them three cheers, to show the folks on shore that there are no hard feelings."

The cheers were given lustily — at least, as lustily as the exhausted condition of the Butterflies would permit. Each member of the defeated club seemed to feel it his duty to banish even the semblance of envy; and it was pleasant to observe how admirably they succeeded.

10

I do not wish my young readers to suppose that Tony's crew felt no disappointment at the result; only that there were no hard feelings, no petty jealousy. They had confidently expected to win the race, even up to the last quarter of a mile of the course; and to have that hope suddenly dashed down, to be beaten when they felt sure of being the victors, was regarded as no trivial misfortune. But so thoroughly had Tony schooled them in the necessity of keeping down any ill will, that I am sure there was not a hard feeling in the club. Perhaps they displayed more disinterestedness in their conduct after the race than they really felt. If they did, it was no great harm, for their motives were good, and they were all struggling to feel what their words and their actions expressed.

"Zephyr, ahoy!" hailed Mr. Hyde, from the Sylph.

"Ay, ay, sir!"

"The prize is ready for the winner."

The oars were dropped into the water again, and the Zephyr pulled up to the judges' boat.

'You have won the prize handsomely. Frank, and

it affords me great pleasure to present it to you,'' said Mr. Hyde, as he handed him a purse containing the prize. " After the noble expressions of kindness on the part of your rival, I am sure the award will awaken no feeling of exultation in the minds of the Zephyrs, and none of envy in the Butterflies. I congratulate you on your victory."

Frank bowed, and thanked the schoolmaster for his hopeful words ; and the Butterflies gave three cheers agair as he took the prize. The Zephyr was then brought alongside her late rival.

" Starboard oars — up ! " said Frank.

" Larboard oars — up ! " added Tony.

" What now, I wonder ? " queried Fred Harper.

" Forward oarsman, step aboard the Butterfly,' continued Frank.

" Forward oarsman, step aboard the Zephyr," said Tony.

Then the next member in each boat was passed over to the other, and so on, till the whole starboard side of the Zephyr was manned by Butterflies, and the larboard side of the Butterfly by Zephyrs

"Ready — up!" said the coxswains, as they proceeded to get under way again.

Thus, with the two clubs fraternally mingled, they slowly pulled towards the nearest shore, while the band played its sweetest strains. The spectators still lingered; and as the boats neared the land, they were greeted with repeated cheers. Then. side by side, they pulled slowly along the shore, within a few rods of the lake's bank, till they reached the Butterflies' house, where they all landed.

And thus ended the famous boat race, over which the boys had been thinking by day and dreaming by night for several weeks. The occasion had passed; and if it was productive of any evil effects in the minds of those who engaged in it, they were more thar balanced by the excellent discipline it afforded. They had learned to look without envy upon those whom superior skill or good fortune had favored, and to feel kindly towards those over whom they had won a victory. It was a lesson which they would all need in the great world, where many a race is run, and where the conqueror is not always gentle towards the conquered — where defeat generates ill will, envy, and hatred.

" A. new commandment I give unto you, that ye love one another," said Jesus — not only love one another when the sky is clear, and the waters are smooth, but when the clouds threaten, and the stormy sea lashes with its fury; not only when the arm of friendship and kindness holds us up, but when all hearts seem cold, when all hands are closed, and all faces frown upon us. It was this divine command that the circumstances of the boat race tended to exemplify; and I am sure that both the conquerors and the conquered were better pre pared for the duty of life than if they had had no such experience.

I do not mean to say that every boat race is a good thing, most especially when it is made to be a gambling speculation by staking money on the result — only that this one was, because those who conducted it made it subservient to the moral progress of the boys.

" Well, Frank, I am glad you won the race," said Tony, with a smile which testified to his sincerity. " Fortune favored us at the bridge, and gave us the opportunity of winning the honors."

10 *

" And the profits too, Tony. Fifty dollars is nothing to us now," added Fred, with a laugh.

" Thank you, Tony," replied Frank. " You are so noble that you almost make me regret we won. But, my dear fellow, you have won a greater victory in your own heart. I can envy you the possession of such noble feelings."

" Pooh, Frank ! "

" I am sure I don't value the victory, because it has been won over you."

" We trained ourselves to *feel right* about the matter whichever way the race went."

" Your heart is so near right that you don't need much training. But it is time for us to return home."

" How about that picnic on the first of May ? "

" My father has consented to it."

" So have our folks ; we will have a glorious time of it. On Saturday afternoon, if you say so, we will visit Centre Island, and set the May pole."

" Agreed."

" But, Frank, school keeps — don't it ? "

" Whew ! does it ? "

"It did last year; but the committee ha;e talked of giving us the day. I hope they will. Ask your father; he is one of them."

"I will. We can get the point settled before Saturday."

"I guess so."

"All aboard!"

The Zephyrs hastened on board, and in a few minites were out of sight. The Butterfly was hauled into her berth, every thing was made "snug" and tidy, and the boys hastened to their several homes. Of course it was not easy for them to drive out of their minds the exciting events of the day, and while all of them, except Tony, were sorry they had lost the race, they had much to console them. They had won a victory over themselves; and the consciousness of this triumph compensated for their disappointment. Each of them, adopting the sentiment of their heroic young leader, thought what a good fellow Frank Sedley was, and *tried* to feel glad that he had won.

There was one of them, however, who did not think much about it after he separated from his companions. Other considerations claimed his attention; and before he reached his humble home, the race was banished from his mind. He had a sick father, and the family had hard work to get along. This was Little Paul.

His mother insisted upon sending him to school while there was any thing left to procure the necessaries of life; and as there was little for him to do at home, he was allowed to join the club, because his parents knew how much he loved the sports on the lake, and that nothing but good influences would be exerted upon him in the association.

Paul Munroe was a good boy, in every sense of the word; and though he had never been able to do much for his parents, they regarded him none the less as one of their choicest blessings. As Tony expressed it, Little Paul's heart was in the right place; and it was a big heart, full of warm blood.

His father sat in an easy chair by the kitchen stove as he entered, and a smile played upon his pale blue lips as his eye met the glance of his loving son.

"Well, Paul, did you win the race?" he asked in feeble tones.

"No, father; the Zephyrs beat. Frank Sedley rather outgeneralled Tony, and his crew were more used to pulling than we. But Frank is a first-rate fellow."

"Isn't Tony?"

"That he is! They are both first-rate fellows; 1 don't know where there are two other such fellows in the world."

"You are right, Paul; they are good boys, and we shall be sorry to take you away from them."

Little Paul looked inquiringly at his father. He had more than once begged to be allowed to work in the Rippleton factories, that he might earn something towards supporting the family; but his parents would never consent to take him away from school and confine him in the noisy, dusty rooms of the mills. His father's words suggested the idea that they had consented to his request, and that he was to be allowed to work for a living.

"'Squire Chase has been here to-day," added Mr. Munroe, sadly.

"Has he? What did he say?" asked Paul, a shade of anxiety gathering upon his fine manly face

"We must leave our house, my son," replied the father, with a sigh.

"Won't he wait?"

"No."

"How did he act while he was here?"

"He was very harsh and unfeeling."

"The villain!" exclaimed Paul, with emphasis, as his cheek reddened with indignation.

"He is a hard man, Paul; but reproaches are of no use. The note is due on the first of May; I cannot pay it, so we must leave the house."

"Where are we to go, father?"

"Your grandfather, who has a large farm in Maine, has written for me to come there; and your mother and I have decided to go."

Paul looked sad at the thought of leaving the pleasant scenes of his early life, and bidding farewell to his cherished friends; but there was no help for it, and he cheerfully yielded to the necessity. It was of no use to think of moving the heart of 'Squire Chase — it was cold, hard, and impenetrable. He was a closefisted lawyer, who had made a handsome fortune in the city by taking advantage of the dis tresses of others, and it was not likely that he, having thus conquered all the nobler impulses of his nature, would have any sympathy for Mr. Munroe in his unfortunate condition.

The poor man had bought the little place he occupied a few years before for seven hundred dollars — paying two hundred down, and giving his note, secured by a mortgage, for the rest. The person of whom he had purchased the place, whose lands joined it, had sold his estate to 'Squire Chase, to whom, also, he had transferred the mortgage. The retired lawyer was not content to remain quiet in his new home, and there repent of his many sins, but immediately got up an immense land speculation, by which he hoped to build a village on his grounds, and thus make another fortune.

Mr. Munroe's little place was in his way. He wanted to run a road over the spot where the house was located, and had proposed to buy it and the land upon which it stood. He offered seven hundred and fifty dollars for it; but it was now worth nine hundred, and Mr. Munroe refused the offer. The 'Squire

was angry at the refusal, and from that time used
all the means in his power to persecute his poor
neighbor.

Then sickness paralyzed the arm of Mr. Munroe,
and he could no longer work. The money he had
saved to pay the note when it should become due
was expended in supporting his family. With utter
ruin staring him full in the face, he sent for 'Squire
Chase, and consented to his offer; but the malicious
wretch would not give even that now; and the land
was so situated as to be of but little value except to
the owner of the Chase estate. The 'Squire was a
bad neighbor, and no one wanted to get near him;
so that Mr. Munroe could not sell to any other
person.

The crafty lawyer knew that the poor man was
fully in his power, and he determined to punish him,
even to his ruin. He hated him because he was
an honest, good man; because his life, even in his
humbler sphere, was a constant reproach to him.
The note would be due on the first of May, and
he had determined to take possession in virtue of
the mortgage.

Poor Paul shed many bitter tears upon his pillow that night; and from the depths of his gentle heart he prayed that God would be very near to his father and mother in the trials and sorrows that were before them.

11

CHAPTER X.

A UNANIMOUS VOTE.

On the following day Little Paul was missed at school, and some anxiety was felt by his companions concerning him. It was feared that the exertion of the race had proved too great for him, and that he was too ill to come out. All the other boys appeared as usual, and none of them seemed to be the worse for the violent exercise they had taken.

Before night, however, they learned that Little Paul was quite well, and had been detained at home to assist his mother. This intelligence removed their anxiety, and their fears lest boat racing should be deemed an improper recreation, and dangerous to the health of the boys. Friday and Saturday passed, and he did not appear at school; but it was said that his mother was very busy, and nothing was thought of the circumstance.

On Saturday afternoon the Butterfly club had assembled in their hall, and were talking over the affairs of the association until the time appointed for the excursion to Centre Island. Little Paul had not come yet, and the boys began to fear that they should be obliged to make the excursion with only five oars on one side.

"What do you suppose is the reason?" asked Dick Chester.

"I have no idea; I hope nothing has happened, for Little Paul has not been absent from school before this season," replied Tony.

"I hope not," added Henry Brown. "Suppose we send a committee to inquire after him."

This was deemed an excellent suggestion, and Henry and Dick were immediately appointed a committee of two, by the "chair," to attend to the matter. They departed upon their mission, and after the boys had wondered a while longer what kept Paul away, another topic was brought up — a matter which was of the deepest interest to the young boatmen, and which had claimed their attention during all their leisure moments for several days.

I say their leisure moments ; for the affairs of the
club were not permitted to interfere with any of the
usual duties of the members.   At home and at
school, it was required that every thing should be
done well, and done promptly.   As may be supposed,
this was not an easy matter for boys whose heads
were full of boats and boating ; and about once a
week the coxswains found it advisable to read a lec-
ture on the necessity of banishing play during work
hours.   " Whatsoever thy hands find to do, do it
with all thy might," was a text so often repeated
that it had virtually become one of the articles of the
constitution.

The boys felt the necessity of following this pre-
cept.   They realized enough of the law of cause and
effect to be aware that, if their home and school
duties were neglected, or slovenly done, boating
would soon obtain a bad reputation ; so both parents
and teacher found that the clubs were a great help
rather than a hinderance in the performance of their
several functions.

So strongly were the Zephyrs impressed with the
necessity of not permitting the club to interfere with

home and school duties, that, at the latter part of
their first season, they had established a rule by
which any member who wilfully neglected his duties
should be, for a certain time, excluded from the club.
And this rule was not a dead letter. One Wednesday forenoon Charles Hardy had wasted his time in
school, and failed in his lessons. On his slate was
found a drawing of a club boat, manned by certain
ill-looking caricatures, which explained the cause of
the defection. An excursion had been planned for
that afternoon, and when Charles presented himself
at the boat house, he was politely informed he could
not go. In vain he pleaded; Fred Harper, who was
coxswain at the time, was very civil and very gentle,
but he was inflexible. And the culprit had the satisfaction of sitting upon a rock on shore, and seeing
what a fine time the, fellows were having.

The effect was decidedly salutary, and another case
of such discipline did not again occur. The boys,
zealous to keep their favorite sport in good repute,
adopted the regulation for the present year, in both
clubs. Without such precautions as these it was
plain that boating would soon become a nuisance,

11 *

which neither parents nor teachers would tolerate. Therefore the members of the clubs made it a point to keep their " voyages," their plans and schemes, out of their minds at times when their heads should be filled with other matters. It was astonishing to what an extent they succeeded; and boys would often be surprised to see how well they can do, if they would only set about it earnestly and with a determination to succeed.

The notable scheme which just now engrossed the attention of the Butterflies was no less than the establishment of a " fleet of boats " upon the lake. The dream of half a dozen boats, under command of Commodore Frank Sedley, manœuvring on the water, performing beautiful evolutions, and doing a hundred things which they could not then define, was so pleasant, so fascinating, that they could not easily give it up.

There would be the commodore in his " flag boat," signalizing the fleet, now bidding them pull in " close order," now ordering a boat out on service, and now sending one to examine a bay or a harbor. And then, if they could only get leave to explore Ripple ton River, how the commander of the squadron would send out a small craft to sound ahead of them, and to buoy off the rocks and shoals, and how the people on the banks of the stream would stare when they saw them moving in sections against the sluggish current! Ah, a fleet of boats was such a brilliant ideal, that I will venture to say more than one of the boys lay awake nights to think about it.

I will not attempt to tell my young friends all the queer fancies concerning the squadron in which they indulged. They were essentially air castles, very beautiful structures, it is true, but as yet they rested only on the clouds. But the means of realizing this magnificent ideal was within their grasp. They had the money to buy the boats, and the only question was, whether George Weston, the "director" of the club, would permit the purchase.

"What have you done about the fleet, Tony?" asked Joseph Hooper.

"I have spoken to my brother about it," replied Tony, with a smile.

"What did he say?"

"He had no objection."

"Hurrah! We shall have the fleet then! And, Tony, we shall go in for having you commodore part of the time."

"That we will!" echoed half a dozen voices.

"You would make as good a commodore as Frank," added Joseph.

"I guess not," answered Tony, modestly. "Didn't you see how slick Frank beat us in the race? If I had followed his tactics, we might have stood some chance, at least."

"Some chance! Didn't we keep ahead of him till we had got almost home?"

"Yes; but that was a part of Frank's tactics. He let us get tired out, and then beat us. But we haven't got the fleet yet, fellows, and we are a pack of fools to count the chickens before they are hatched."

"You said George has no objections," replied Joseph, glancing anxiously at Tony.

"He has not, but he wants to consult Captain Sedley before he consents."

The boys looked a little disconcerted at this intelligence, and a momentary silence ensued.

" Do you think he will object, Tony ? " asked one.

" I am pretty sure he will not."

" Have you said any thing to Frank about it ? "

" Yes; and he says the Zephyrs will put their money with ours, if we get the fleet."

" Hurrah!   I *know* his father will consent ! "

" I have even got a hint from him that he should not object," added Tony, very quietly.

" That is glorious!   We shall certainly have the fleet then ! " shouted Joseph Hooper.

" I am pretty sure there will be no trouble about it.   Almost every body is willing to admit now that the clubs are a good thing; that they keep the fellows out of mischief, and stimulate them to do their duty at home and at school.   So much for our strict regulations.   If we can get more boats, and form more clubs, every body concerned will be the better for it."

" That's the idea."

" We can get four small boats for our money — can't we ? " asked one of the boys.

" Frank thought we had better get different sized boats," replied Tony.

"For different kinds of service," added Joseph, demurely.

"Say, one eight-oar boat, one six-oar, and two four-oar," said Tony.

"That would be first rate! Then we could take in twenty-two fellows."

"Twenty-three; the commodore would not be the coxswain of any boat, but command the whole."

The boys grew so nervous and excited during this fine discussion, that they could hardly keep their seats. In imagination the fleet was already afloat, and the broad pennant of Commodore Sedley was flying on board the Zephyr.

"How long before we can get the boats, Tony?" asked a little fellow, his eyes snapping with delight at the glorious anticipation.

"Perhaps they can be bought ready made. We need not wait for new ones. In a few weeks, at least before vacation —— Hallo, Paul! I am glad you have come."

Little Paul looked very sad as he entered Butter-fly Hall. With a faint smile he received the greet ings of his friends.

"All aboard! shouted Tony, as he rose from his chair. "You haven't got your uniform on, Paul.'

"I can't go with you, Tony," replied Little Paul, in a gloomy tone.

"Not go with us! Why not? What is the matter?"

"I must leave the club too," he added, in a husky voice.

"Leave the club!"

"We are going to move Down East."

"That's too bad!"

All the boys gathered round Little Paul, and there was a troubled look upon their countenances.

"We cannot stay here any longer," continued the poor boy, as he dashed a tear from his eye.

It was evident to all that some misfortune had overtaken the Munroe family, and Little Paul's sorrows excited the deepest interest and sympathy.

Without any solicitation on the part of his companions, the little fellow told them the story of his father's trials, and the reason why he was compelled 'o leave Rippleton.

"When is the money due, Paul?" asked Tony

" On the first of May. My father has no money and he cannot pay the note."

" How much did you say it was ? "

" Five hundred dollars.   It is a great sum for us "

" My father says 'Squire Chase is not any better than he ought to be," added Dick Chester, who had returned with Little Paul.

" He is a very hard man," replied Paul.   " But I must go home again.   I shall see you before I leave town ; " and the poor fellow turned away to hide his tears.

" Poor Little Paul ! " said Tony, when he had gone.

" How I pity him ! " added Henry Brown.

" So do I," reiterated Joseph Hooper.

" How much do you pity him, fellows ? " asked Tony, seating himself in his arm chair.

" So much that we would help him if we could," answered Henry.

" You *can* help him."

A deep silence ensued.

" Have you the nerve to make a great sacrifice Butterflies ? " exclaimed Tony, with energy.

" We have."

" I move you, Mr. Chairman, that our four hundred dollars be applied to the relief of Little Paul's father," said Henry Brown, catching Tony's idea.

" Second the motion," added Dick Chester, promptly.

" Bravo !" shouted Tony, slapping the table with his fist. " That's what I call noble ! But before we do it, just think what a fine thing the fleet would be. It is a great sacrifice."

" Question !" called Joseph Hooper.

" Think well, fellows," said Tony. " Any remarks upon the subject will be in order. It is a great question, and ought not to be hastily decided."

" Question !" shouted the whole club, wildly.

" Those in favor of applying the four hundred dollars to the relief of Mr. Munroe will signify it," said Tony.

" All up !"

" *It is a unanimous vote !*"

12

CHAPTER XI.

BETTER TO GIVE THAN RECEIVE.

"ALL aboard!" shouted Tony, as soon as he had declared the vote; and the boys hurried into the boat to be in readiness to join the Zephyr, which was already upon the lake.

Tony's spirits were unusually buoyant. The sympathy and coöperation of the club in regard to Little Paul's father was in the highest degree grateful to his feelings. Perhaps his companions did not so cheerfully resign the project of the fleet; perhaps they had acted upon the impulse of the moment; but they were all to experience the benefit of doing a good deed, of sacrificing their own gratification for the happiness of others. Tony felt better for the sacrifice they had made, and probably the rest of them shared his feelings. He was satisfied that they did not fully realize what they had done, and with the determination to take a fit opportunity to talk over the matter with them, he took his place in the boat.

The Zephyrs were laying on their oars, waiting for the Butterfly when she backed out of the boat house.

"You are late, Tony, which is rather odd for you," said Frank.

"We had a little business to attend to, which detained us," replied Tony; "and while we are here we may as well tell you about it. We have voted our money away."

"For the fleet?"

"No; we have given that up."

"Indeed! Given it up?" exclaimed Frank, not a little surprised at this declaration.

"Fact, Frank!"

"Something new has turned up, then?"

"Let us lash boats to keep us from drifting apart, and I will tell you all about it."

The two boats were fastened together fore and aft, and Tony proceeded to tell the story of Little Paul's father. He spoke loud enough for all the Zephyrs to hear him and as his heart warmed towards Mr. Munroe in his misfortunes, his eyes dilated, and his gestures were as apt and energetic as though he had been an orator all his lifetime.

"I see what you have done with your money," said Frank, as the speaker paused at the close of the narrative. "It was like you, Tony — noble and generous!"

"We gave all our money for the relief of Mr. Munroe; but I didn't even suggest the thing to the fellows. Henry Brown made the motion, and it was a unanimous vote."

"Bravo, Butterflies!"

"Have you given up the fleet?" asked Tim Bunker, whose face was the only one which did not glow with satisfaction.

"Yes."

"There is more fun in helping a poor man out of trouble than in working a fleet," added Henry Brown.

"So I say!" put in Dick Chester.

"Humph!" grunted Tim.

"But, Tony, you said the note was five hundred dollars — didn't you?" asked Frank.

"I did."

"And you have only four hundred?"

"That's all;" and Tony's eyes rekindled with delight at the anticipation of what the Zephyrs would do.

"You hear that, fellows."

"Would a motion be in order now?" asked Charles Hardy.

"Hold your tongue, you fool!" said Tim Bunker, in a low tone. "We can get another boat with our money, and you shall be coxswain of it."

Charles looked at him.

"A motion would be in order; at least we can *make* it in order," replied Frank.

But Charles hesitated. The tempting offer of Tim, the absurdity of which he did not stop to consider, conquered his first impulse.

"I move you we appropriate one hundred dollars to put with the Butterfly's money for Mr. Munroe," said William Bright, and Charles had lost the honor of making the motion.

"Second the motion," added Fred Harper.

12 *

" Those in favor of giving our money to Mr. Munroe will signify it."

"Vote against it," said Tim; and Charles accepted the suggestion.

" Ten ; it is a vote, though not unanimous," continued Frank, as he cast a reproachful glance at his friend who had voted against the proposition.

He was not surprised to see Tim Bunker vote against it ; but that Charles should receive the advice of such a counsellor, and such advice too, was calculated to alarm him. His friend had but little firmness, and was perhaps more likely to be led away by bad influences than any other member of the club. He was sorry to see Tim exhibiting his dogged disposition, but more sorry to see Charles so much under his control.

" Hurrah !" shouted Tony, when the vote was declared. " Let us send up to Mr. Munroe, and tell him what we have done, and get Little Paul. They won't want him now."

" But, Tony, you forget that our doings must be approved by our directors," said Frank.

" I'll risk them."

"It would be better to have every thing right be-fore we promise Mr. Munroe."

"So it would. Is your father at home?"

"I believe so."

"George is, and it won't take five minutes to ob-tain his consent. Let go the fasts forward," said Tony, as he cast off the line astern.

"We will go ashore, and try to find my father," added Frank. "Ready — pull!"

Away dashed the Zephyr towards her boat house, while the Butterfly came about so that Tony could leap on shore.

Of course both Captain Sedley and George Wes ton were surprised at the sudden action of the clubs; but the deed was too noble, too honorable to their kind hearts to want their sanction, and it was readily given. In less than half an hour the boats were pulling towards a convenient landing-place near Mr. Munroe's house.

The poor man was confounded when the committee of two from each club waited upon him and stated their business. His eyes filled with tears, and he and Little Paul wept together.

But Mr. Munroe could not think of aking the money at first. He declared that he would suffer any thing rather than deprive the boys of the gratification which their money would purchase.

"We are a little selfish about it, sir," said Tony. "We want to keep Paul among us."

"That's the idea," added Henry Brown, who was his colleague on the committee.

"I can't take your money, boys," replied Mr. Munroe, firmly.

"You will oblige us very much by taking it. My brother and Captain Sedley both know what we are about. I am sure we shall feel happier in letting you have this money than we should be made by any thing it will buy. It was a unanimous vote in our club."

"Noble little fellows!" exclaimed Mr. Munroe, with a fresh burst of tears, as he grasped the hand of Tony.

The matter was argued for some time longer, and finally compromised by Mr. Munroe's agreeing to accept the money as a loan.

The notes were drawn up and signed by the poor

man, whose heart was filled to overflowing with gratitude at this unexpected relief.

"Now you will let Paul come with us — won't **you,** Mr. Munroe?" asked Tony.

"Certainly; and I shall never cease to thank God that he has found such noble and true friends," replied the poor man; and as they took their leave, he warmly pressed the hands of each member of the committee.

"Cheer up, Paul; don't be down-hearted. It is all right now," said Tony.

"I can't be lively," replied Little Paul, whose sadness cast a shade upon the enjoyment of the others.

"Why not, Paul?"

"I feel so sad; and your goodness to my poor father overcomes me."

"Never mind that, Paul; cheer up, and we will have a glorious time."

But Little Paul's feelings were too strong and deep to be easily subdued. His pride seemed to be wounded by the events of the day, and when they reached Centre Island, he told Tory how badly he felt about his father being the recipient of their charity, as he called it.

"Charity, Paul!" exclaimed the noble little fellow. "Look here;" and he pulled the note he had received from Mr. Munroe out of his pocket. "Do you call this charity?"

"Perhaps he can never pay you; at least, it will be a long time."

"No matter; it is a fair trade. We lent him the money."

And Tony argued the point with as much skill as a lawyer would have done, and finally so far succeeded in convincing Paul, that his face brightened with a cheerful smile, and he joined with hearty zest in the preparations for the May day picnic.

A long spruce pole, which had been prepared for the occasion by Uncle Ben, was towed to the island by the Zephyr, and erected in a convenient place. The brushwood in the grove was cleared from the ground, the large stones were rolled out of the way, and were used in constructing a pier for convenience in landing. When their labors

were concluded it was nearly dark, and the boats
pulled for home, each member of the clubs antici
pating a glorious time on the approaching holiday
for such the committee had decided the First ot
May should be.

CHAPTER XII

FIRST OF MAY.

MAY day came — warm, bright, and beautiful. At six o'clock in the morning the Zephyr and the Butterfly were manned, and the boys went over to the island to trim the May pole with evergreen and flowers. The Sylph was degraded for the time into a "freighting vessel," and under command of Uncle Ben conveyed to the island chairs and settees for the use of the guests, tables for the feast, music stands for the band, and other articles required for the occasion.

About nine o'clock the guests began to arrive, and were conveyed to the island by the two club boats — the Sylph having gone down to Rippleton after the band. The Sedleys, the Westons, Mr. Hyde, the parents of all the members of the clubs who could attend, all the boys and girls of the school, and a few gentlemen and ladies from the village who had manifested a warm interest in the welfare of the two associations. composed the party ; and before ten they were all conveyed to the scene of the festival.

" Have you got them all, Frank ? " asked Captain Sedley, as the coxswain was ordering his crew ashore.

" All but the Munroes, and the Butterflies are going for them by and by."

" Tom is hoisting the signal," added Captain Sedley, pointing to a blue flag on the shore, which the gardener had been directed to hoist when any one wished to go to the island.

" We will go, Frank," said Tony; and away dashed the boat towards the main shore.

" Ah, my Butterflies," said a voice, as they approached the landing.

" Mr. Walker ! " exclaimed Tony. " Ready — up ! Now let us give him three cheers. I was afraid he would not come."

The salute was given, and acknowledged by Mr. Walker.

13

"I am glad to see you again, my brave boy," said the gentleman, as he grasped Tony's hand.

"I was afraid you would not deem our invitation worth accepting."

"I would not have missed of coming for the world, my young friend. Here is Mrs. Walker; you know her."

Tony shook hands with the lady, and she said a great many very pretty things to him, which made the gallant little hero blush like a rose in June, and stammer so that he could hardly make them understand him.

"Shall I help you into the boat, Mrs. Walker?" said Tony.

"You shall, my little gallant; though I shall not be so glad to get into it as I was the other day."

The boat put off again, and Mr. and Mrs. Walker were filled with admiration of the excellent discipline of the rowers. They were warmly greeted by the party at the island, and lustily cheered by the crew of the Zephyr, which was again manned for the purpose of giving their liberal friend this compli mentary salute.

"Off again, my lads?" asked Mr. Walker, as the Butterflies prepared to go for the Munroe family.

Captain Sedle: explained to him the nature of their present errand; and, of course, the warm-hearted gentleman found renewed occasion to applaud the nobleness of Tony and his companions. He could hardly find terms sufficiently strong to express his sense of admiration, especially when he learned the sacrifice which they had made.

"A fleet of boats!" exclaimed he. "If it would raise up such boys as these, it ought to be procured at the public expense. Thank God! I am rich."

"I understand you, Mr. Walker," replied Captain Sedley; "but I beg you will not let your generosity do any thing more for the boys."

"Captain Sedley, I *love* those boys! They are good boys, and good boys are a scarcity nowadays. There is nothing too good for them."

"You are enthusiastic."

"But I tell you, sir, there are no such boys as those in the world!" exclaimed Mr. Walker, with a gesture of earnestness.

"O, yes, sir; I presume, under the same disci-pline, other boys would be the same."

" Then let them have the same discipline."

" It would cost a fortune. It is a very extrav-
agant recreation, this boating."

" But it makes men of them. I read the constitution of the clubs, and Tony tells me it is carried
out to the fullest extent."

" No doubt of it. There are boys among them,
who, under other circumstances, would be bad boys.
I am satisfied the club keeps them true to themselves
and their duty."

" That's just my idea ; and as these noble-hearted
little fellows have bestowed the money I gave them
in such a commendable manner, I mean to give them
as much more."

" That was my own feeling about the matter ; but
I do not think it is a good plan to make good all
they sacrifice. This fleet scheme was a cherished
project, and it was noble in them to give it up that
they might do a good deed."

" Noble ! It was heroic — I was just going to
use a stronger word."

" It is good for them to practise self-denial. That
is all that makes the deed a worthy one."

" Exactly so."

" Therefore, my friend, we will not say any thing more about the fleet at present."

" But if they bear it well, if they don't repent what they have done, why, I should not value one or two thousand dollars. Besides, it might be the means of bringing a large number of boys within the pale of good influences."

" That is my own view; and by and by we will talk more of the matter."

Captain Sedley then introduced Mr. Walker to the company, and the benevolent gentleman took a great deal of pains to inform himself in relation to the influence of the boat clubs upon the boys. He asked a great many questions of their parents, and of Mr. Hyde, the teacher. They all agreed that the young men were the better for the associations; that the discipline was very useful, and the physical exercise very healthy; but some of them were afraid their sons would acquire such a taste for the water as to create a desire to follow the seas. But few of them considered boating, under the discipline of the clubs, a dangerous recreation; so that the only

real objection was the tendency to produce long·
ings for

> " A life on the ocean wave,
> A home on the rolling deep."

Mr. Walker tried to make the sceptical ones be·
lieve that Wood Lake was so entirely different from
the "rolling deep" as scarcely to suggest the idea
of a ship, or of the ocean.   But the disadvantages
were trivial compared with the benefits which all
acknowledged to have derived from the associations,
even independently of the libraries, the lectures, and
the debating societies at the halls.

Tony and his companions soon returned with the
Munroe family, who were cordially received by the
guests.   Captain Sedley expressed his sympathy for
the poor man, regretting that he had not known his
situation before.

"I would have bought your place myself rather
than have had you sacrifice your property to the
cupidity of such a man," said he.

"You are very good, sir," replied Mr. Munroe;
"but I had not the courage to state my circumstances to any body. 'Squire Chase is a very hard

man; even when I paid him the money, which the kindness of the boys enabled me to do, he was so angry that he could scarcely contain himself. He swore at me, and vowed he would have vengeance."

"He must be a very disagreeable neighbor."

"He is, indeed."

"On with the dance!" shouted Frank, in the most exuberant spirits; and the rich and the poor man dropped the subject.

The boys and girls had formed a line round the May pole, and the band commenced playing a very lively air. As the inspiring notes struck their ears, they began to jump and caper about, taking all sorts of fantastic steps, which it would have puzzled a French dancing master to define and classify. Most of the boys and girls knew nothing of dancing, as an art; but I venture to say they enjoyed themselves quite as much as though they had been perfectly proficient in all the fashionable waltzes, polkas, and redowas. Their hearts danced with gladness, and their steps were altogether *impromptu*.

Then came the ceremony of crowning the Queen of May, in the person of Mary Weston, which was

performed in the most gallant style by Frank Sed-
.ey. Another dance succeeded, and then came the
feast. A great many good things were eaten, a
great many fine things said, and a great many patri-
otic and complimentary toasts were drank. The
band played " Hail Columbia," " Yankee Doodle,"
and many other spirited tunes, and Mr. Walker was
very much astonished, as well as amused, to hear
some of the boys make speeches, flowery and fine,
which had evidently been prepared for the occasion,
when they were " called up " by the toasts.

After the feast was over, the party divided itself
into little knots for social recreation. Frank and
Mary Weston took a walk on the beach, and the rest
of the boys and girls climbed over the rocks, amused
themselves in the swing which Uncle Ben had put
up, or wandered in the grove. Boys and girls always enjoy themselves at such seasons, and my
young readers need not be told that they all had a
" first-rate time."

I do not mean all; for two members of the Zephyr
Club had wandered away from the rest of the party
to the north side of the island. They were concealed

from view by a large rock; but if any one had observed them, he could not have failed to see that they were exceptions to the general rule — that they were not happy. The two boys were Charles Hardy and Tim Bunker. Frank had been pained to notice that an unnatural intimacy had been growing up between them for several days; and he had already begun to fear that it was in the heart of Tim to lead his weak-minded associate astray.

"Now, let's see how much there is in it," said Tim.

"I am afraid to open it," replied Charles, as he glanced nervously over the rocks.

"Git out!"

"I am doing wrong, Tim; I feel it here." And Charles placed his hand upon his heart.

"Humph!" sneered Tim. "Give it to me, and I will open it."

"We ought not to open it," replied Charles, putting his hand into his pocket, and again glancing over the top of the rocks. "Besides, Tim, you promised to be a good boy when we let you into the club."

"I mean to have a good time. We might have

had if you fellows hadn't given away all that money."

" I didn't do it."

" I know you didn't, but the rest on 'em did ; so it's all the same. They are a set of canting pups, and for my part I'm tired on 'em. Frank Sedley don't lord it over me much longer, you better believe ! And you are a fool if you let him snub you as he does every day."

" I don't mean to," answered Charles. " I believe the fellows all hate me, or they would have made me coxswain before this time."

" Of course they would. They hate you, Charley : I heard Frank Sedley say as much as that the other day."

" He did ? "

" Of course he did."

" I wouldn't have thought that of him," said Charles, his eye kindling with anger.

" Let's have the purse, Charley."

Charles hesitated ; but the struggle was soon over in his bosom, and he took from his pocket a silken purse and handed it to Tim.

"We are doing wrong, Tim," said he, as a twinge of conscience brought to his mind a realizing sense of his position. "Give me back the purse, and I will try to find the owner."

"No, you don't!" replied Tim, as he opened one end of the purse and took therefrom a roll of bank bills, which he proceeded to count.

"Do give it back to me! I am sure the owner has missed it by this time."

"No matter if he has; he won't get it again in a hurry," answered the Bunker, coolly. "Sixty dollars in bills! Good!"

"Give it to me, or I will go to Captain Sedley and tell him you have it."

"Will you?"

"I will."

"If you do, I'll smash your head," said Tim, looking fiercely at him. "Don't be a fool! With this money we can have a first-rate time, and nobody will be any the wiser for it."

"I am afraid we shall be found out."

Probably Charles was more afraid of that than of the wicked act which he had permitted himself to think of doing. He had found the purse on the beach a little while before. When he had told Tim of it, the reckless fellow, still the same person as before, notwithstanding his promises and his altered demeanor, had led him over to this retired spot in order to get possession of the purse.

"Nonsense! Nobody will suspect you," replied Tim, as he poured out the silver and gold in the other end of the purse.

"I never did such a thing in my life."

"No matter; there must be a beginning to every thing."

"What would my mother say?"

"She will say you are a clever fellow if you don't get found out. Eleven dollars and a quarter in specie! That makes seventy-one twenty-five — don't it?"

"Yes."

"All right! We will just dig a little hole here, and put the purse into it," continued Tim, as he scooped out a hole in the sand, and dropped the ill-gotten treasure into it.

Filling up the hole, he placed a large flat stone

upon the spot,, which further secured the purse, and concealed the fact that the sand had been disturbed.

"I am sure we shall get found out," said Charles, trembling with apprehension.

"Nonsense! Keep a stiff upper lip; don't stop to think, and all will go well. But, my hearty, if you peach on me, I give you my word, I will take your life before you are one month older — do you hear?" And Tim's fierce looks gave force to his words. "Now, we will go back to the rest on 'em before they miss us. Mind you don't say any thing. nor look any thing."

Charles followed Tim back to the other side of the island, and both of them joined the sports of the day. The afternoon passed away, and nothing was said of the purse. The owner had not missed it, and Tim congratulated himself on the circumstance. Charles tried to be joyous, and though he did not feel so, he acted it so well that no one suspected him of harboring so vile a sin within his bosom.

"All aboard!" said Frank, and the band commenced playing "Home, Sweet Home."

14

In due time the party were all transported to the shore, and every body went home highly delighted with the day's amusements. The Zephyr was housed, and the crew dismissed, but not a word was said about the purse.

CHAPTER XIII.

THE LIGHTHOUSE.

Durīng the month of May, the members of the two clubs continued to spend many of their leisure hours on the lake; but my young friends must not suppose that life was to them a continuous holiday; and, because these books are devoted chiefly to their doings on the water, that boating was the only, or the principal business that occupied them. They had their school duties to perform, their errands to do, wood to split, yards to sweep; in short, they had to do just like other boys. A portion of Wednesday and Saturday afternoon, and of their other holidays, was given to these aquatic sports; so that they were really on the lake but a small part of the time. Probably, if they had spent all their leisure in the boats, the exercise would have lost its attractions, besides interfering very much with their home and school affairs. Pleasures, to be enjoyed, should be partaken of in moderation. Boys get sick of most sports in a short time, because they indulge in them too freely.

Nothing specially worthy of note occurred in either club till near the end of the month of May. The intimacy between Charles Hardy and Tim Bunker was observed to increase, though no one had any suspicion of the secret which had cemented the bond of their union.

The lost purse was the property of Mr. Walker. At a subsequent visit to Rippleton, he had mentioned his loss, but he had no idea where he had dropped it. Tim congratulated his still unwilling confederate on the success of his villany. Mr. Walker did not even know whether he had lost his money in the town or not; so, of course, he had no suspicion of them.

"You are a first-rate fellow, Charley, but you are too chickenish by half," said Tim Bunker.

"I don't feel right about it, and I wish I had given up the purse when I found it."

"Pooh!"

" I meant to do so."

" I know you did. You were just fool enough to do such a thing. If it hadn't been for me, you would have done it."

" O, I wish I had ! "

" Don't be a fool, Charley.

" I would give the world to feel as I felt before I did this thing."

" Don't think any more about it."

" I can't help thinking. It worries me nights."

" Go to sleep then."

" I can't. What would Frank say if he knew it ?"

" Humph ! Frank again ! "

" They would turn me out of the club."

" You are no worse than any of the rest of them."

" They wouldn't steal," replied Charles, warmly.

" Don't you believe it. If I should tell all I know about some of them, they wouldn't be safe where they are, let me tell you."

" What do you know, Tim ? "

" I don't choose to tell."

Charles found some satisfaction in this indefinite accusation ; but it was not enough to quiet his

14 *

troubled conscience. Life seemed different to him since he had stolen the purse — he had not got far enough in wickedness yet to believe that it was *not* stolen. He felt guilty, and his sense of guilt followed him wherever he went. He could not shake it off. Every body seemed to look reproachfully at him. He avoided his companions in the club when not on duty with them. He began to hate Frank Sedley, though he could not tell the reason. William Bright, who was now the coxswain, Frank's term having expired, was a very strict disciplinarian, and the guilty boy had grown very impatient of restraint. He was surly and ill natured when the coxswain rebuked him, even in the kindest tones. Every thing went wrong with him, for the worm was gnawing at his heart.

"Won't you tell *me*, Tim?" asked he, in reply to Tim's remark.

"Not now, Charley; one of these days you shall know all about it."

"I am afraid we shall both get turned out of the club."

"No we shan't if we do —— But no matter."

" What would you do, Tim ? "

" Never mind now, Charley. I have a plan in my head. Captain Sedley told me the other day if I didn't behave better I should be turned out."

" Then you will be."

" I don't care if I am. If they turn me out, they will make a mistake ; that's all."

There was something mysterious in the words of the Bunker which excited the curiosity of Charles. He could not help wondering what he would do. Tim had so much resolution he was sure it was not an idle boast.

" I know what I am about," continued Tim, with a wise look.

" Captain Sedley says you still associate with your old companions," added Charles.

" What if I do ? "

" That would be ground enough for turning you out."

" Would it ? They are better fellows than you long faces, and you will say so when you know them," replied Tim, speaking as though it were a settled fact that he would know them by and by.

This conversation occurred one Wednesday afternoon, as the two boys were on their way to the boat
house. On their arrival, Tim was informed by Captain Sedley, who was apparently there for that purpose, that he was expelled from the club. It was
sudden and unexpected, and had been done by the
director without any action on the part of the club.

"What for?" asked Tim, in surly tones.

"I find that you still associate with your old
companions, which is sufficient proof that you don't
mean to reform," answered the director.

"I don't care," growled Tim, as he turned on his
heel and walked out of the hall.

Charles Hardy was then called aside by Captain
Sedley, who kindly pointed out to him the danger
he incurred in associating with such a boy as Tim.

"I would not have kept company with him if
he had not been a member of the club," replied
Charles.

"He was admitted to the club on the supposition
that he intended to be a better boy."

"I was opposed to admitting him,' answered
Charles, rather sulkily.

"I was very willing the boy should have a fair chance to reform; but when it became apparent that he did not mean to do better, I could no longer permit him to endanger the moral welfare of the club. We have been satisfied for some time; and most of the boys, after giving him a fair trial, avoided him as much as possible when they saw what he meant. But you have been growing more and more intimate with him every day. Why, it was only last night that he was seen with some twenty or thirty of his old companions. They seemed to be in consultation about something. Perhaps you were with them."

"No, sir; I was not."

"I am glad you were not. I caution you to avoid them."

"I will, sir," replied Charles, meekly; and he meant what he said.

"I am glad to hear you say so; I was afraid you had known too much of Tim Bunker," said the director, as he walked towards his house.

Charles entered the hall, and took his seat.

"Those in favor of admitting Samuel Preston to

the club will signify it," said William, as soon as he was in his place.

Eleven hands were raised, and the new member, who stood by the window waiting the result, was declared to be admitted. The constitution was then read to him, and he signed it; after which the club embarked for an excursion up to the strait, where they had agreed to meet the Butterfly.

The particular object of this visit was to erect a lighthouse on Curtis Island, a small, rocky place, separated from the main shore by " Calrow Strait," which the readers of " The Boat Club " will remember. The navigation of this portion of the lake was considered very difficult, especially through the narrow passage, and it was thought to be absolutely necessary to have a lighthouse, maugre the fact that the boats always sailed by day. But as neither craft was insured, it was necessary to use extraordinary precautions !

A working party of half a dozen was detailed from each boat, consisting of the stoutest boys, who were landed upon the island. Materials were immediately gathered and the foundation laid. The structure was to be a simple round tower, as high as the patience of the workmen would permit them to build it.

In a short time all the rocks on the island had been used up, and the lighthouse was only two feet high ; but this contingency had been anticipated, and provisions made for supplying more stone. A large rock was attached to the long painter of the Butterfly, and she was moored at a safe distance from the island, while her remaining crew were transferred to the Zephyr.

A rude raft, which had been provided by Tony, was towed to the shore, where an abundance of rocks were to be had. It was their intention to load it with "lighthouse material," and tow it to the island. It required all their skill to accomplish this object, for the raft was a most ungainly thing to manage. The Zephyr was so long that they could not row round so as to bring the raft alongside the bank, and when they attempted to push it in, the paint, and even the planks of the boat, were endangered.

" Can't get it in — can we ?" said Charles Hardy, after several unsuccessful attempts.

" There is no such word as fail," replied William ~ Bring me the long painter."

The coxswain unfastened the tow line of the raft, and tied the painter to it.

"Bowman, stand by with the boathook, ready to land."

"Ay, ay!"

"Now, pull steady; be careful she does not grind on the rocks; easy, there. Four of you jump ashore."

The four forward rowers obeyed the command.

"Now pass this line ashore, and let them pull in on the raft," continued William.

"Hurrah! there she is!" shouted Frank. "That was done handsomely!"

"We could have done it before, if we had only thought of it," replied William, laughing. "Now put out the fenders, and haul the boat alongside the raft."

Four more of the boys were sent on shore to help roll down the rocks, and two were ordered upon the raft to place them. A great deal of hard work was done in a very short time; but, as it was play, no one minded it, as probably some of them would if the labor had been for any useful purpose. In due time the raft was loaded with all it would carry, and the boys were ordered into the boat again.

The raft proved to be a very obstinate sailer. After a deal of hard tugging at the oars, they succeeded in getting it under a tolerable headway; but the tow line was not properly attached, and it " heeled over" so as to be in danger of " spilling " its load into the lake. Prudence and good management, however, on the part of the coxswain, conveyed it in safety to the island, and its freight soon became " part and parcel " of the lighthouse.

Two or three loads more were brought, after the lesson of experience obtained in getting the first, with but comparatively little difficulty; and at six o'clock the tower received its capstone at a height of six feet from the ground, and twelve from the water.

The lighthouse was then inaugurated by a volley of cheers. A hollow pumpkin of last year's growth, containing a lighted candle, was placed upon the apex; and then the boats departed for home. At eight o'clock, when the darkness had gathered upon the lake, they saw the light from their homes, and had the satisfaction of knowing that the light keeper was watchful of the safety of vessels in those waters.

As Charles Hardy passed through the grove on his way home, after the club separated, he met Tim Bunker, who was apparently awaiting his coming.

CHAPTER XIV.

THE CONSPIRACY.

"WELL, Charley, my pipe is out," said Tim Bunker, as he joined his late associate in the club.

"It was rather sudden," replied Charles, disconcerted by the meeting, for he had actually made up his mind to keep out of Tim's way. "I didn't expect any such thing."

"I did; I knew old Sedley meant to get rid of me.

Tim always knew every thing after it was done. He was a very profound prophet, but he had sense enough to keep his predictions to himself

"You did not say so," added Charles, who gave the Bunker credit for all the sagacity he claimed.

"It was no use; it would only have frightened you, and you are chickenish enough without any help. But no matter, Charley; for my part, I am glad he turned me out. He only saved me the trouble of getting out myself."

" Did you really mean to leave ? "

" To be sure I did."

" What for ? "

" Because I didn't like the company, to say noth·
ing of being nosed round by Frank Sedley, Bill
Bright, or whoever happened to be coxswain.   If you
had been coxswain, Charley, I wouldn't minded it,"
replied Tim, adroitly.

" But I wouldn't nose the fellows round," replied
Charles, tickled with Tim's compliment.

" I know you wouldn't ; but they wouldn't make
you the coxswain.   They hate you too much for
that."

" It is strange they haven't elected me," said
Charles, musing.

" That's a fact !   You know more about a boat
than three quarters of them."

" I ought to."

" And you do."

Charles had by this time forgotten the promise he
had made to Captain Sedley — forgotten the good
resolution he had made to himself.   Tim's flat·
tery had produced its desired effect, and all the

ground which the Bunker had lost was now re-gained.

" I am sorry they urned you out, Tim," said he.

" I am glad of it. They will turn you out next, Charley."

" Me ! "

" Yes."

" Why should they ? "

" Because they don't like you."

" They wouldn't do that."

"Don't you believe it," replied Tim, shaking his head, and putting on a very wise look. " I'll bet they'll turn you out in less than a month."

" Do you know any thing about it ? "

" Not much."

They had now reached the end of the grove, and Tim suggested that they should take seats and " talk over matters." Charles readily assented, and they seated themselves by the margin of the lake.

" What do you know, Tim ? " asked Charles, his curiosity very much excited.

" I only know that they don't like you, and they mean to turn you out."

15 *

"I don't believe it."

" Do you mean to tell me I lie ? "

" No, no ; only I can't think they would turn *me* out."

" I heard Frank say as much," replied Tim, indifferently.

" Did you ? "

" To be sure I did."

Charles stopped to think how mean it was of Frank to try to get him out of the club ; how hypocritical he was, to treat him as a friend when he meant to injure him. It did not occur to him that Tim had told a falsehood, though it was generally believed that he had as lief tell a lie as the truth.

" You are a fool if you let them kick you out, as they did me," continued Tim.

" What can I do ? "

" Leave yourself."

" Next week is vacation ; and we have laid out some first-rate fun."

" There will be no fun, let me tell you."

" What do you mean, Tim ? "

" If you want to be the coxswain of a boat as

good as the Zephyr next week, only say the word, replied Tim, slapping him on the back.

"How can that be?" asked Charles, looking with surprise at his companion.

"And you shall have as good a crew as the Zephyr; better fellers than they are, too."

"I don't understand you."

"You shall in due time."

"Tell me what you mean, Tim."

"Will you join us?"

"Tell me about it, first."

"And let you blow the whole thing?"

"I won't say a word."

"Will you promise not to say any thing?"

"Yes."

"Will you swear it?"

Tim had read a great many "yellow covered" books in his time, in which tall buccaneers with long beards and bloodshot eyes required their victims to "swear," and he seemed to attach some importance to the ceremony. Charles "swore," though with considerable reluctance, not to reveal the secret, when 't should be imparted to him.

' " You must join our society, now."

" Society ? "

" Yes ; we meet to-night at eight o'clock, in the woods back of my house."

" What sort of a society is it, Tim?" asked Charles, with a great many misgivings.

" That you shall learn when we meet. Will you come ? "

" My father won't let me go out in the evening."

" Run out, then."

Tim suggested various expedients for deceiving his parents, and finally Charles promised to attend the meeting.

" You haven't told me the secret yet."

" The society is going to camp on Centre Island next week, and we are going to take the Zephyr and the Butterfly along with us."

" Take them ?   How are you going to get them ? "

" Why, take them, you fool ! "

" Do you mean to steal them ? "

" Humph !   We mean to *take* them."

" But do you suppose Captain Sedley and George Weston will let you keep them ? "

" They can't help themselves. We shall take the Sylph, and every other boat on the lake, with us, so that no one can reach us. Do you understand it ? "

" I do ; but how long do you mean to stay there ? "

" All the week."

" And sleep on the ground ? "

" We can have a tent."

" How will you live ? "

" We shall carry off enough to eat beforehand. Then, you see, we can sail as much as we please, and have a first-rate time on the island. I shall be coxswain of one boat, and you shall of the other if you like."

" But we shall have to come home some time "

" In about a week."

" What would my father do to me then ? "

" Nothing if you manage right. If he offers to, just tell him you will run away and go to sea. He won't do nothing then."

" I don't know about that."

" He won't kill you, any how. And you will have a week's fun, such as you never had before in your life."

"The Zephyrs won't have any thing to do with me after that."

"They hate you, Charley, and all they want is to get you out of the club. You are a fool if you don't leave yourself."

Charles paused to consider the precious scheme which had thus been revealed to him. To spend a week on the island, and not only be his own master for that time, but command one of the boats, pleased him very much. It was so romantic, and so grateful to his vanity, that he was tempted to comply with the offer. But then the scheme was full of peril. He would "lose caste" with the Zephyrs; though, if Tim's statement was true, he was already sacrificed. His father would punish him severely; but perhaps Tim's suggestion would be available, and he knew his mother would be so glad to see him when he returned, that she would save him from the effects of his father's anger. His conscience assured him, too, that it would be wrong for him to engage in such a piece of treachery towards his friends; but Tim declared they were not his friends — that they meant to ruin him.

Thus he reasoned over the matter, and thus he got rid of the objections as fast as they occurred to him. While he was thinking about it, Tim continued to describe in glowing colors the fun they could have; occasionally relating some adventure of "Mike Martin," "Dick Turpin," or other villain, whose lives and exploits were the only literature he ever read.

But Charles could not fall at once. There were some difficulties which he could not get over. It was wrong to do as Tim proposed; it was so written on his soul. The "still small voice" could not be silenced. As fast as he reconciled one objection, another came up, and something in his bosom kept saying, "You must not do it."

The more he thought, the more imperative was the command. "Run away as fast you can!" said the voice within him. "You are tempted; flee from the temptation."

"I guess I won't join you, Tim," said he.

"You won't, eh?" replied Tim, with a sneer.

"I think not; I don't believe it is right. But I won't say any thing about it."

"I rather guess you won't. It wouldn't be safe for you to do so."

"I won't, upon my honor, Tim," replied Charles, rising from his seat, and edging away from his dangerous companion.

"Look here, Charley Hardy; in one word, you've got to join the Rovers."

"The what?"

"That's the name of the society," answered Tim, who had mentioned it without intending to do so.

It was certainly a piratical appellation, and Charles was not prepossessed by it in favor of the society. It had a ring of bold and daring deeds, and his studies had not prepared him to entertain a very high opinion of Tim's heroes, Dick Turpin and Captain Kidd.

"You can't back out now, Master Hardy," continued Tim.

"I don't want to join you, but I won't say a word."

"Very well, my fine fellow!" and Tim rose and walked away towards home.

Charles did not like this. He was afraid of Tim; afraid that some terrible thing would happen to him if he did not keep on the right side of him.

Like thousands of others, he had not the courage to do his duty, and leave the consequences to take care of themselves. He was more afraid of the Bunker than of the frowns of an accusing conscience.

"I say, Tim!" he called.

"Well, what you want *now*?" replied Tim, stopping.

"Suppose I don't join?"

"Then you will be in Rippleton jail before tomorrow night; that's all."

"What for?"

"No matter; if you come to the meeting to-night, all right; if you don't — Rippleton jail;" and Tim hastened away, heedless of Charles's calls.

"Rippleton jail! What could he mean by that?" He felt guilty, and his heart beat so violently that he could hardly breathe. The stolen purse, which still lay buried on Centre Island, seemed to haunt him, and with that he immediately connected Tim's dreadful threat. His confederate meant to charge him with stealing it. It was all very plain, and his conscience told him how justly he would be accused. He could not go to jail innocent, as Tony had,

16

and be borne home in triumph from the court by the boat club.

His frame trembled with emotion; and he knew not what to do. There was a right way and a wrong way for him to proceed — the path of duty and the path of error.

"I will go to Captain Sedley and tell him all about it," said he to himself, "and tell him that they mean to steal the boats."

This was the path of duty; but he had not the courage to walk in it. He would be despised even then, and Tim Bunker would certainly be revenged if he did.

"I *will* go;" and he actually walked a short distance towards Captain Sedley's house; but his courage failed him; he dared not do right, and that evening he joined the 'Rovers."

Poor Charles!

CHAPTER XV.

THE "ROVERS."

AFTER Charles Hardy had joined the " Rovers' ' band, which was composed of the original Bunkers, with others whom Tim had collected together, his conscience proved less troublesome. The first wrong step taken, the second follows with less compunction, and so on, till the moral sense is completely blunted.

At the meeting he was informed by Tim that he had been admitted to the society on account of his knowledge of boats. They could not get along without such a fellow; and he was accordingly appointed "master of marine," and second in command to Tim himself. These honors and compliments reconciled him to the society of the Rovers, and he began to exhibit his energy of purpose in directing the details of the next week's operations.

Saturday was appointed as the day for stocking the island with provisions and other necessaries ready for the reception of the entire party on Sunday night. Tim and Charles were to attend to this duty in person.

"Meet me at eight o'clock in the morning over by Joe Braman's landing, Charley, and —— "

"But school keeps ; I can't go till afternoon."

"And then the Zephyrs will see what we are about."

"I can't help it."

"Yes you can; can't you ' hook Jack ' ? "

"I dare not."

"Humph ! You are an idiot ! Tell the fellows to-morrow that you are going over to your uncle's, and they will tell the master."

Charles consented, after some argument.

"I will get Joe's boat, and we can pull off to the island and get the money."

"Where will you buy the things ? "

"We must go down to Rippleton. You must get some, and I will get some. We will buy them at different stores, so no one will know but what they are for the folks."

" And the tent ? "

" We will get a piece of cotton cloth for that, and some needles and thread. Leave all that to me Now, be on hand in season."

" One thing, Tim : I may be seen in Rippleton."

" No matter if you are. Bluff 'em off if they say any thing."

The Rovers were to " rendezvous " — Tim had found this word in the " Adventures of the Bold Buccaneer " — at nine o'clock on Sunday evening at the wood. The arrangements were all completed, and the band dispersed.

On Saturday Charles was true to his appointment, and met Tim on the north side of the lake. The money was procured, and the provisions were safely deposited in the boat. It is true, Charles was so much embarrassed that he well nigh betrayed the existence of the plot to the shopkeepers; and he was very glad when this part of the business was done.

Then a new difficulty presented itself. Suppose the Zephyrs should visit Centre Island that afternoon and discover the stores ! They had not thought

16 *

of this before, and the risk was too great to be incurred. They decided to conceal their stores on the main shore till night, and then carry them off. A convenient place was found for this purpose, and the articles were landed.

They then repaired to the island to mature their plans.

"Now, where shall we pitch the tent?" asked Charles, when they landed.

"On the high ground near the beach."

"We have no poles. Here is the May pole; that will do for one."

"We can't pitch the tent, soldier fashion. We must drive down four forked stakes; then put poles on the forks, and cover the whole with cloth."

"But where are the stakes and the poles?"

"We can cut them in the woods. We will get Joe Braman's axe, and do it this forenoon."

"Suppose they should make a raft, and come off to us?" suggested Charles.

"We have two fast boats, and can easily keep out of their way," replied Tin . "If they want to fight, we can beat them off."

Charles did not approve of fighting, and though it would be bad policy. Tim was tolerably tractable now that he was having his own way, and was not very strenuous in support of his own pugnacious views. When their plans were fully digested they left the island to prepare the stakes. Before noon they separated, and the truant returned home about the usual time.

That afternoon he joined the Zephyrs in an excursion up the lake, and another lighthouse was erected in the vicinity of a dangerous reef.

" What shall we do next week ? " asked Charles, as they were returning home.

" We are going up the river," replied Frank. " My father has consented to it."

" Has he ? That will be first rate."

" And so has George Weston."

Charles relapsed into deep thought. He was thinking how much better he could enjoy himself with good boys than with such fellows as the Rovers; for, though he was " master of marine " among them, he could not help acknowledging to himself that they were not pleasant companions. They used

profane and vulgar language ; were always disposed
to quarrel. Disputes which were settled peaceably
in the clubs were decided by a fight among the
Rovers; and the ambitious " master" had many misgivings as to his ability to control them. Tim could
manage them very well; for, if one was turbulent,
he struck him and knocked him down; and Charles
had not the brute courage to do this.

"What are you thinking about, Charley?" asked
Frank, pleasantly.

"Nothing," replied Charles, promptly, as he tried
to laugh.

"You act rather queerly this afternoon; just as
though you had something on your mind."

"O, no; nothing of the kind."

"I hope you don't regret the expulsion of Tim
Bunker."

"Certainly not."

Charles tried to be gay after that; but he could
not. There was a weight upon his soul which bore
him down, and he felt like a criminal in the presence
of his companions. He was glad when the club
landed, and the members separated — glad to get

away from them, for their happy, innocent faces were a constant reproach to him.

Sunday was a day of rest; but every moment of it was burdened with a sin against God and against himself. Every moment that he delayed to repent was plunging him deeper and deeper in error and crime. Strangely enough, the minister preached a sermon about the Prodigal Son; and the vivid picture he drew of the return of the erring wanderer so deeply affected the youthful delinquent that he fully resolved to do his duty, and expose the Rovers' scheme.

The money had been spent in part; but, if they sent him to jail, it would be better than to continue in wickedness. Then he thought what Captain Sedley would say to him; that the club would despise him; and that he would not be permitted to join the sports of the coming week — to say nothing of being put in prison.

But his duty was plain, and he had resolved to do it. He had decided to suffer the penalty of his transgression, whatever it might be, and get back again into the right path as soon as he could.

Happy would it have been for him had he done so. On his way home from church he unfortunately met Tim Bunker, who had evidently placed himself in his way to confirm his fidelity to the Rovers.

Tim saw that he was meditating something dangerous to the success of his scheme. Charles was cold and distant. He appeared to have lost his enthusiasm.

"If you play us false, it will be all up with you," said Tim, in a low, determined tone. " I can prove that you stole the purse. That's all."

It was enough to overthrow all Charles's good resolution. His fickle mind, his shallow principle, gave way. Stifling his convictions of duty, and silencing the " still small voice," he went home : and there was no joy in heaven over the returning prodigal.

"Charles," said his father, sternly, as he entered the house, " you were not at school yesterday ! "

" I got late, and did not like to go," whined he.

" Where were you ? "

" Down at the village."

" Go to your room, and don't leave it without permission."

Charles obeyed. The consequences of his error were already beginning to overtake him. His father joined him soon after, and talked to him very severely. He was really alarmed, for Captain Sedley had given him a hint concerning his son's intimacy with Tim Bunker.

Charles was not permitted to leave his room that afternoon, and his supper was sent up to him; but his mother brought it, and consoled him in his troubles — promising to prevent his father from punishing him any more.

" Now, go to bed, Charley; never do so again, and it will be all right to-morrow," said the weak mother, as she took her leave.

But Charles did not go to bed. The family retired early ; and, taking his great coat on his arm, he stole noiselessly out of the house. At nine o'clock he was at the rendezvous of the Rovers.

It was not deemed prudent to put their plans in execution till a later hour ; and the band dispersed, with instructions to meet again in an hour at Flat Rock, where the boats would be in readiness to take them off to the island.

Tim and Charles, with four others, immediately repaired to the place where Joe Braman's boat, which had been hired for the enterprise, was concealed. Seating themselves in it, they waited till the hour had expired, and then, with muffled oars, pulled up to the Butterfly's house.

The doors which opened out upon the lake were not fastened, and an entrance was readily effected. The boat was loosed, pushed out into the lake without noise, and towed down to the Zephyr's house. But here the doors were found to be fastened; and one of the boys had to enter by a window, and draw the bolt. The boat was then secured without difficulty.

"Now, Charley, you get into the Zephyr with two fellows, and tow the Sylph off," said Tim, in a whisper.

"Shan't I get my crew first?"

"Just as you like."

Charles and his two companions got into the Zephyr and worked her down to the rock, where he received his crew. It was found then that some of the Rovers had not yet made their appearance, so that there were only ten boys to each boat.

Although the success of the criminal undertaking required the utmost caution, Charles found his command were disposed to be very boisterous, and all his efforts would hardly keep them quiet. After some trouble he got away from the shore; but his crew, from the want of discipline, were utterly incapable of pulling in concert. They had not taken three strokes before they were all in confusion — tumbling off the thwarts, knocking each other in the back, and each swearing at and abusing his companions.

" Hold your jaw, there ! " called Tim Bunker, in a low tone, from the Butterfly.

" Cease rowing ! " said Charles.

But they would not " cease rowing," and the prospect was that a general fight would soon ensue in spite of all the coxswain's efforts to restore order. At last Tim came alongside, and rapping two or three of the turbulent Rovers over the head with a boathook, he succeeded in quieting them.

After several attempts Charles got them so they could pull without knocking each other out of the boat ; but he was heartily disgusted with his crew,

17

and would gladly have escaped from them, even if Rippleton Jail had yawned to receive him. After half a dozen trials he placed the Zephyr alongside the Sylph, let go her moorings, and took her in tow The Rovers then pulled for the island; but the pas sage thither was long and difficult.

CHAPTER XVI.

THE CAMP ON THE ISLAND.

As the crew of the Zephyr tugged at their oars, their imperfect discipline imposing double labor upon them, Charles had an opportunity to consider his position. The bright color of romance which his fancy had given to the enterprise was gone. The night air was cold and damp, and his companions in error were repulsive to him. There was no pleasure in commanding such a motley crew of ill-natured and quarrelsome bullies, and if it had been possible, he would have fled from them. Who plunges into vice may find himself in a snare from which he cannot escape though he would.

At last they reached the island, and the Sylph was anchored near the shore. There was a great deal of hard work to be done; but each of the Rovers seemed to expect the others would do it.

"Now, Charley, every thing is right so far," said Tim Bunker, whose party had just drawn Joe Braman's boat upon the beach.

"Every thing is wrong," Charles wanted to say; but Tim was too powerful to be lightly offended.

"I can do nothing with such a crew as that," whined he. "They won't mind, and every fellow wants his own way."

"Hit 'em, if they don't mind," replied Tim.

"I think we had better spend an hour in drilling them. We can't handle the boat as it is."

"We must get the tents up before we do any thing else. You go after the stakes and poles and I will get the provisions."

Before the crews returned to the boats, Tim made a little speech to them upon the necessity of order; promising, if any boy did not obey, he would thrash him "within an inch of his life."

"Now tumble into the boats, and, Charley, if any feller don't do what you tell him, let me know it, and I will lick him for you."

"All aboard!" said Charles.

"Where are we going now?" asked one of his crew.

"No matter; all you have got to do is to obey orders," replied Charles, sharply.

"Say that again!" said the fellow, with an oath, as he doubled up his fist, and menaced the unfortunate coxswain with a thrashing.

"Hallo, Tim!" shouted Charles, who dared not venture to carry out the Bunker's summary policy.

"What's the row?" said Tim, as he hastened to the spot.

"I can't do any thing with this crew; here is a fellow shaking his fist in my face."

"Let him be civil then," added the refractory Rover.

"It was you, was it, Barney?" said Tim, as he stepped into the boat.

"I'll bet it was," replied the fellow, standing upon the defensive.

"Take that, then," continued the "chief," as he brought his fist down upon the rebel with such force that he tumbled over the side of the boat into the water. "You want to get up a mutiny — don't you?"

The fellow scrambled ashore, wet through and shivering with cold.

17 *

" You'll catch it for that, Tim Bunker!" growled Barney.

" I'll teach you to mind. Now, Charley, put off, and don't be so stiff with them yet. They are not such chicken-hearted pups as the Zephyrs, I can tell you ; " and Tim stepped ashore.

" Take your oars ; if you only do as I tell you, we shall get along very well," said Charles. " We can't do any thing unless you mind."

He then showed them how to get their oars out, and how to start together ; but they did not feel interest enough in the process to pay much attention to what he said, and several ineffectual attempts were made before they got a fair start.

" Hallo ! Ain't you goin to take me ? " shouted Barney, from the shore, as they were leaving.

" Will you obey orders ? "

" Yes ; but I won't be kicked."

" Nobody wants to kick you," replied Charles, who, deeming that the rebel had made a satisfactory concession, put back after him.

" This ducking will be the death of me," said Barney, as he got into the boat.

"A little hard pulling will warm you, and when we get back, we shall make a fire on the island," answered Charles, in a conciliatory tone. "Now, ready — pull!"

The Rovers worked better now, and the Zephyr moved with tolerable rapidity towards the shore; but it was very dark under the shadow of the trees, and Charles could not readily find the place where the materials for the tent had been concealed. Each of the crew thought he knew more about the business than the coxswain; and in the scrape the Zephyr was run aground, heeled over on one side, and filled half full of water.

It required some time to bail her out; but it was accomplished at last, the stakes and poles put on board, and they rowed off to the island again. Tim had arrived before him, and had landed the stores.

"Where are the matches, Tim?" asked Charles.

"What are you going to do?"

"Make a fire."

"What for?"

"Some of us are wet, and we can't see to put up the tents without it."

" But a fire will betray us."

" What matter? We are safe from pursuit."

" Go it, then," replied Tim, as he handed Charles
a bunch of matches.

The fire was kindled, and it cast a cheerful light
over the scene of their operations.

" Now, Rovers, form a ring round the fire," said
Tim, " and we will fix things for the future."

The boys obeyed this order, though Barney, in
consideration of his uncomfortable condition, was
permitted to lie down before the fire and dry his
clothes.

" I am the chief of the band; I suppose that is
understood," continued Tim.

" Yes," they all replied.

" And that Charley Hardy is second in command.
He can handle a boat, and the rest of you can't."

" I don't know about that," interposed one of
them. " He upset the boat on the beach."

" That was because the crew did not obey orders,"
replied Charles.

" He is second in command," replied Tim. " Do
you agree to that ? "

" Yes," answered several, who were willing to fol-
ow the lead of the chief.

"Very well; I shall command one **party,** and
Charley the other; each in his own boat and on the
island. Now we will divide each party into two
squads, or watches."

"What for?" asked Barney.

"To keep watch, and do any duty that may be
wanted of them."

Tim had got this idea of an organization from his
piratical literature. Indeed, the plan of encamping
upon the island was an humble imitation of a party
of buccaneers who had fortified one of the smallest
of the islands in the West Indies. The whole scheme
was one of the natural consequences of reading bad
books, in which the most dissolute, depraved, and
wicked men are made to appear as heroes, whose
lives and characters are worthy of emulation.

Such books fill boys' heads with absurd, not to say
wicked ideas. I have observed their influence in the
course of ten years' experience with boys; and when
I see one who has named his sled "Blackbeard,"
' Black Cruiser," "Red Rover," or any such names,

I am sure he has been reading about the pirates, and nas got a taste for their wild and daring exploits—for their deeds of blood and rapine.   One of the truant officers of Boston, whose duty it is to hunt up runaway boys, related to me a remarkable instance of the influence of improper books.   A few years ago, two truant boys were missed by their parents. They did not return to their homes at night, and it was discovered that one of them had stolen a large sum of money from his father.   A careful search was instituted, and the young reprobates were traced to a town about ten miles from the city, where they were found encamped in the woods.   They had purchased several pistols with their money, and confessed their intention of becoming highwaymen !   It was ascertained that they had been reading the adventures of Dick Turpin, and other noted highwaymen, which had given them this singular and dangerous taste for a life in violation of the laws of God and man.   My young readers will see where Tim got his ideas, and I hope they will shun books which narrate the exploits of pirates and robbers.

Two officers were chosen in each band to command

the squads. Tim was shrewd enough to know that the more offices he created, the more friends he would insure — members who would stand by him in trial and difficulty. In Charles's band, one of these offices was given to the turbulent Barney; his fidelity was thus secured, and past differences reconciled.

"Now, Charley, my crew shall put up one tent, and yours the other."

"Very well," replied Charles, who derived a certain feeling of security from the organization which had just been completed, and he began to feel more at home.

The stakes were driven down, and the poles placed upon the forks; but sewing the cloth together for the covering was found to be so tedious a job that it was abandoned. The strips were drawn over the frame of the tent, and fastened by driving pins through it into the ground. Then it was found that there was only cloth enough to cover one tent. Tim's calculations had been defective.

"Here's a pretty fix," said Tim.

"I have it," replied Charles. "Come with me, Barney, and we will have the best tent of the two."

Charles led the way to the Sylph, and getting on board of her by the aid of one of the boats, they proceeded to unbend her sails.

"Bravo! Charley," said Barney. "That's a good idea; but why can't some of us sleep in this bit of a cuddy house?"

"So we can. Here is Uncle Ben's boat cloak, which will make a first-rate bed. Don't say a word about it, though, and you and I can have it all to ourselves."

The sails were carried ashore, and were ample covering for the tent. Dry leaves, which covered the ground, were then gathered up and put inside for their bed.

"Now, Tim, they are finished, and for one, I begin to feel sleepy," said Charles.

"We can't all sleep, you know," added the prudent chief.

"Why not?"

"We must set a watch."

"I am too sleepy to watch," said Charles, with a long gape. The clock has just struck one."

"You needn't watch, you are the second in command."

"I see," replied Charles, standing upon his dignity.

"There are four watches, and each must do duty two hours a night. Who shall keep the first watch?"

"I will," said Barney.

"Good! You must keep the fire going, and have an eye to both sides of the island."

"Ay, ay."

"And you must go down to the boats every time the clock strikes, to see if they are all right. If they should get adrift, you know, our game would be up."

"I'll see to it."

"At three o'clock, you must call the watch that is to relieve you."

"Who will that be?"

"I" volunteered the three other officers of the wat. hes, in concert.

"Ben, you shall relieve him. If any thing happens, call me."

Tim and his followers then retired to their tent, and buried themselves in the leaves. Charles ordered

18

.hose of his band who were not on duty to "turn in ;" saying that he wanted to warm his feet. The Rovers were so fatigued by their unusual labors that they soon fell asleep, and Charles then repaired to the little cabin of the Sylph. Arranging the cloak for his bed, he wrapped himself up in his great-coat and lay down.

Fatigued as he was, he could not go to sleep. The novelty of his situation, and the guilt, now that the excitement was over, which oppressed his conscience, banished that rest his exhausted frame required. He heard the village clock strike two and three ; and then he rose, unable to endure the reproaches of his own heart.

"What a fool I am !" he exclaimed to himself; and a flood of tears came to his relief. "To desert my warm bed, my happy home, the friendship of my club, for such a set of fellows as this ! O, how I wish I had not come !"

Leaving the cabin, he seated himself in the stern sheets of the boat. The bright stars had disappeared, and the sky was veiled in deep black clouds. The wind blew very fresh from the north-east, and he was certain that a severe storm was approaching. He wept bitterly when he thought of the gloomy prospect.

He had repented his folly, and would have given the world to get away from the island. Ah, a lucky thought! He could escape! The Rovers were all asleep; the fresh breeze would soon drive the Sylph to the land, and he could return home, and perhaps not be missed. It was an easy thing; and without further reflection, he unfastened the cable, and dropped it overboard.

The Sylph immediately commenced drifting away from the island. Taking the helm, he put her before the wind, and was gratified to observe that she made very good headway.

The clock struck four, and he heard the footsteps of the watch upon the shore.

" Boat adrift ! " shouted Ben, who was the officer of the watch.

The words were repeated several times, and in a few moments he heard Tim's voice summoning his crew. Then the Butterfly dashed down upon him,

and his hopes died within him. But he had the
presence of mind to crawl back again to the cabin ;
and when Tim came on board, he had the appearance of being sound asleep, so that the chief did not
suspect his treachery.

CHAPTER XVII

THE ESCAPE.

'MONDAY was a cold, dreary, disagreeable day. The wind continued north-east; a fine, drizzly rain was falling, and a thick fog had settled over the lake, which effectually concealed the camp of the Rovers from the main shore.

An excursion had been planned for the day by the two boat clubs; but the weather was so unpropitious that it was abandoned. About nine o'clock, however, the members of the clubs began to assemble at their halls in search of such recreation as could be found in doors.

Frank opened the Zephyr's boat house as usual, and great was his dismay when he discovered that the boat was not in its berth. Calling Uncle Ben from the stable, he announced to him the astounding intelligence that the Zephyr had been stolen!

18 *

" What does it mean, Uncle Ben ? " he asked, in deep anxiety.

" I can't tell you, Frank ; only, as you say, it has been stolen.   It couldn't have broken adrift."

" Of course not ; and one of the windows is open."

" That accounts for it," replied Uncle Ben, as he walked down the boat house and looked out upon the lake.   " I will take the Sylph and hunt it up."

" Let me go with you, Uncle Ben."

" My eyes ! but the Sylph is gone too ! " exclaimed the veteran, as he perceived the moorings afloat where she usually lay.

" Strange, isn't it ? "

Uncle Ben scratched his head, and did not know what to make of it.

" Here comes Tony, running with all his might," continued Frank.   " What's the matter, Tony ? "

" Some body has stolen the Butterfly ! " gasped Tony, out of breath."

" And the Zephyr and the Sylph ! "

Several of the members of the club now arrived, and the matter was thoroughly discussed.

" Who do you suppose stole them ? " said Frank.

" Who ? why, Tim Bunker of course," replied Fred.

" But he must have had some help."

" Perhaps not; he has done it to be revenged, because your father turned him out of the club."

" Very likely."

" May be he'll smash them up," suggested William Bright.

" Have you seen any thing of Charles this morning ? " asked Mr. Hardy, entering the boat house at this moment.

" No, sir.'

" He did not sleep at home last night."

The Zephyrs looked at each other with astonishment, and most of them, probably, connected him with the disappearance of the boats. His intimacy with Tim Bunker created a great many painful misgivings, especially when Mr. Hardy told them that his son had played truant on Saturday; and one of the boys had heard of his being seen with Tim on that day. Various other facts were elicited, which threw additional light upon the loss of the boats.

Mr. Hardy was in great distress. It was clear that his son had wandered farther from the path of truth than he had ever suspected.

Frank had gone up to the house to inform his father of the loss of the boats, and Captain Sedley soon joined the party. He sympathized deeply with Mr. Hardy, and was satisfied that his son could not be far off. It was impossible to search the lake, as there were no boats for the purpose.

As nothing could be done at present on the lake, Captain Sedley ordered his horse, with the intention of driving round it in search of the fugitive and of the boats. Mr. Hardy was invited to go with him.

On their arrival at Rippleton they found that Tim Bunker was missing, as well as a great many other boys. They continued to examine the shores of the lake till they reached Joe Braman's house, on the north side.

Captain Sedley inquired for his boat; and Joe, after trying to evade the truth, confessed that he had let it to Tim for a week, but did not know where he had gone with it. They were sure then that the boys were engaged in some mad enterprise;

and at about eleven o'clock the two gentlemen
reached home, without having obtained any intelligence of Charles.

"Have you discovered any thing, Ben?" asked
Captain Sedley.

"Yes, sir; I heard voices in the direction of Centre Island."

"They are there, then," replied Captain Sedley,
as he repaired to the boat house.

About one o'clock the fog lifted, and revealed to
the astonished party the camp of the Rovers. A
large fire burned near the two tents, around which
the boys were gathered, for the weather was so
inclement as to render Tim's enterprise any thing
but romantic.

The Sylph, the two club boats, and Joe Braman's
" gondola " lay near the shore, apparently uninjured.

" This is a mad frolic," said Captain Sedley; " but
we may be thankful it is no worse."

" My boy in company with such young scoun-
drels!" added Mr. Hardy, bitterly.

" He is sick of them and the adventure 1 will
warrant."

" I hope so."

" Charles never did like Tim Bunker," suggested
Frank.

" What is to be done ? " asked Mr. Hardy.

" We can do nothing ; they have all the boats.
They have managed well, and we are helpless."

" Can't we build a raft, father ? " added Frank.

" If we did, they would take to the boats and keep
out of our way. Go to the house, Frank, and bring
me the spy glass. We will examine them a little
more closely."

" They'll get enough on't afore to-morrow," said
Uncle Ben.

" It will cure them of camping out."

" Tim said, the last time he was with us, that we
ought to camp out," added William.

" The best way is to let them have it out till they
are sick on't," continued Uncle Ben. " It won't hurt
'em ; they won't get the scurvy."

Captain Sedley took the glass on Frank's return,
and examined the camp. By its aid he obtained a
very correct idea of their encampment. The Rovers
were at dinner, and he recognized Charles Hardy and

several of his companions. The glass was taken by
several of the party; and, after this examination
even Mr. Hardy concluded that it was best to make
a merit of necessity, and let the foolish boys have out
their frolic.

Soon after, the Rovers took to the boats, and
pulled up the lake. Then, the anxious party on
shore discovered that Charles was in command of
the Zephyr. With the help of the spy glass they
were able to form a very correct idea of the state
of feeling on board the boats. There was a great
deal of quarrelling in both; and after they had been
out half an hour a regular fight occurred in the
Zephyr.

About five o'clock they returned to the island, and
before dark it began to rain. All the evening a
great fire blazed on the island; but the frail tents
of the Rovers must have been entirely inadequate to
protect them from the severity of the weather.

At nine o'clock the Zephyrs, who had spent the
evening in the hall, went home, leaving Uncle Ben,
who had been deputed by Captain Sedley to watch
the Rovers, still gazing through his night glass at

the camp fires on the island. Soon after, discordant cries were wafted over the waters, and it was plain to the veteran that there was "trouble in the camp." The sounds seemed to indicate that a fight was in progress. After a time, however, all was quiet again, and the old sailor sought his bed.

During the night it cleared off, and Tuesday was a bright, pleasant day. It was found in the morning that one of the tents had been moved away from the other. About nine o'clock all the Rovers gathered on the beach; but they were divided into two parties, and there seemed to be a violent dispute between them. One of the parties, as they attempted to get into the Zephyr, was assaulted by the other, and a fight ensued, in which neither gained a victory. Then a parley, and each party took one of the boats and pulled away from the island. It was observed that Charles was no longer the coxswain. He seemed to have lost the favor of his companions, and several of them were seen to kick and strike him.

The boats went in different directions — the Zephyr pulling towards Rippleton. When her crew observed the party who were watching them from the shore, they commenced cheering lustily, and the coxswain, out of bravado, steered towards them.

" Who is he ? " asked Frank.

" It is Barney Ropes," replied Tony. " He is as big a rascal as there is out of jail."

" Here they come."

" Suppose we give them a volley of stones," suggested Fred Harper.

" No ! " said Frank, firmly.

The boat was pulling parallel with the shore, and not more than ten rods from it. The Rovers yelled, and indulged freely in coarse and abusive language, as they approached. Charles Hardy, with averted face, was pulling the forward oar ; but not one of his former companions hailed him. They pitied him ; they were sure, when they saw his sad countenance, that he was suffering intensely.

Suddenly Charles dropped his oar, and stood up.

" See ! Tim Bunker ! " shouted he, pointing to the opposite side of the lake.

All the crew turned their eyes that way, and Charles, seizing his opportunity, sprang with a long leap into the water.

19

The act was so sudden that the crew could not, for a moment, recover from their astonishment, and Charles struck out lustily for the shore.

"After him!" shouted Barney; and his companions bent upon their oars.

But their excitement threw them into confusion. They lost the stroke, and Barney was such a bungler himself that he could not get the boat about.

"Bravo, Charley!" shouted the Zephyrs.

"Let him go," said Barney, when he realized that the fugitive was beyond his reach; and, rallying his crew, he retreated towards the island.

"Hurrah, Charley! You are safe," said Tony, as he waded into the water to help him ashore.

Charles was so much exhausted when he reached the land that he could not speak. Captain Sedley, who had observed the occurrence from his library window, hastened down to the beach.

The penitent Zephyr, in his agony, threw himself on his knees before him, and in piteous, broken accents besought his pardon. Captain Sedley was deeply moved, and they all realized that " the way of the transgressor is hard."

Tl e sufferer was kindly conveyed to his home by Captain Sedley, and his father and mother were too glad at his return to reproach him for his conduct. When he had changed his clothes, and his emotion had in some degree subsided, he confessed his errors, and solemnly promised never to wander from the right path again. And he was in earnest; he felt all he said in the depths of his soul. He had suffered intensely during his transgression; and his friends were satisfied that he had not sinned from the love of sin. He had been led away by Tim Bunker, and bitter had been the consequences of his error. He had been punished enough, — the sin had been its own punishment, — and his father and his club freely forgave him. He was not a hardened boy, and it was probable that his experience with the Rovers would prove a more salutary correction than any penalty that could be inflicted.

From Charles all the particulars of the "frolic" were obtained. After his unsuccessful attempt to escape in the Sylph, Tim had compelled him to stay in his tent; and worn out with fatigue and suffering. he had slept till nearly nine o'clock. He had passed the day in a state bordering upon misery. At night a dispute had occurred, ending in a fight, in which his lieutenant, Barney, had led on the Zephyr party. The result was a separation, and Charles, deprived of Tim's aid, could no longer sustain himself. Barney usurped his command, and treated him in a most shameful manner.

O, how bitterly did he repent his folly and wickedness! When they were about to embark, he attempted to go over to Tim's party. Barney resented the attempt, and another fight ensued. Then he was kicked into the boat, for his chief could not spare so able an oarsman.

His mental anguish was so great that he could no longer endure it; and, in desperation, he had made his escape, as we have narrated. His case was a hopeful one, and his father cheerfully remitted to Mr. Walker the amount contained in the lost purse, with the mortifying confession of his son's guilt.

CHAPTER XVIII.

WRECK OF THE BUTTERFLY.

THE next day Mr. Walker arrived at Rippleton himself. The noble-hearted gentleman seemed to be in unusually good spirits, and the boys noticed that he and Captain Sedley often exchanged significant glances. They were all satisfied that something was about to happen, but they could not imagine what.

Frank and Tony had been requested to invite their friends to assemble at Zephyr Hall at nine o'clock, on Wednesday morning; so that when Mr. Walker entered the hall with Captain Sedley, the whole school, to the number of over seventy, were gathered there.

Charles Hardy was there with the rest; but he seemed to be a different boy. He had lost that forwardness which had often rendered him a disagreeable companion. He had been forgiven; Mr. Walker

19 *

had spoken to him very kindly, and all his friends
treated him as though nothing had happened; but
for all this, he could not feel right. His sufferings
were not yet ended; repentance will not banish at
once the remembrance of former sin and error. There
was a deep feeling of commiseration manifested
towards him by his associates. He was to them the
returned prodigal, and they would fain have killed
the fatted calf in honor of his happy restoration.

The Zephyrs and the Butterflies wore their uni-
forms, and Mr. Walker was so excited that all the
boys were sure a good time was before them;
though, as the boats had not yet been recovered,
they were at a loss to determine the nature of the
sports to which they had been invited.

The Rovers still maintained themselves on the
island. The rupture between Tim and Barney had
evidently been healed; for both parties seemed to
mingle as though nothing had occurred to mar their
harmonious action.

The boys at the boat house were not kept long in
suspense in relation to their day's sport. Captain
Sedley formed them into a procession, when all had

arrived, and, after appointing Fred Harper chief
marshal, directed them to march down to Rippleton, cross the river, and halt upon the other side till
he came.

When they reached the place they found Uncle
Ben there, and soon after were joined by Captain
Sedley and Mr. Walker.

" Follow us," said the former, as he led the way
down to a little inlet of the lake, whose waters were
nearly enclosed by the land.

" Hurrah !" shouted Fred Harper, suddenly, when
he obtained a view of the inlet, and the cry was
taken up by the whole party.

" The fleet ! The fleet ! " was passed from mouth
to mouth ; and unable to control their excitement,
they broke their ranks and ran with all their might
down to the water's side.

Resting gracefully, like so many swans, on the
bright waters of the inlet, lay five beautiful club
boats. They were of different sizes, and fore and
aft floated their flags to the gentle breeze.

I will not attempt to describe the wild delight of
the boys when they beheld the splendid boats. The

bright vision of a fleet, which they had so cheerfully abandoned to be enabled to do a good and generous deed, was realized. Here was the fleet, far surpassing in grandeur their most magnificent ideal.

Five boats! And the Zephyr and the Butterfly would make seven!

"You have done this!" exclaimed Frank, as Mr. Walker approached.

"Your father and I together did it. Now, boys, if you will form a ring we will explain."

"Three cheers for Mr. Walker first," suggested Tony.

They were given, and three more for Captain Sedley.

"My lads, I heard all about your giving up the fleet to help Mr. Munroe out of trouble. It was noble — heroic; and I have since taken pains to inform myself as to the manner in which you conducted yourself after the brave sacrifice. As far as I can learn, not a regret has been expressed at the mode in which your money was applied. Here is your reward," and he pointed to the boats. "They are the gift of Captain Sedley and myself. I am sorry that these Rovers have taken your other boats; but it enables us to observe the difference between good boys and bad boys. Nay, Master Hardy, you need not .blush; for, though 'you have erred, you have behaved heroically; you risked your life to escape from them; you are forgiven."

This speech was received with shouts of applause, and Charles Hardy stepped forward with tears in his eyes to thank the kind gentleman for his generosity towards him.

" Now, boys," said Captain Sedley, " we are going to recover the lost boats.

" Hurrah!" shouted all the boys.

" Two of these boats, you perceive, carry twelve oars each. The crew of the Zephyr will man the Bluebird."

The Zephyrs obeyed the order.

" The crew of the Butterfly will man the Rainbow," continued Captain Sedley.

The Butterflies seated themselves in the new boat.

" This is merely a temporary arrangement, and when we get the other boats, we shall organize anew. We want practised oarsmen for our present service.

While we are absent, Uncle Ben will instruct the rest of the boys in rowing.

Captain Sedley and Mr. Walker then seated themselves in the stern sheets of the Bluebird.

"Now pull for Centre Island," said the former. "Tony, you will follow us."

The two boats darted out of the inlet, leaving Uncle Ben in charge of the " recruits."

The Lily and the Dart were eight-oar boats, while the Dip carried only four, and was designed as a " tender " for the fleet. Uncle Ben assigned places to the boys, though there were about thirty left after the oars were all manned. After an hour's drilling, he got the crews so they could work together, and the boats were then employed in conveying the rest of the party over to the boat house. The others in their turn were instructed; and before noon Uncle Ben had rendered them tolerably proficient in the art of rowing.

When the Bluebird reached Centre Island, Tim had just embarked in the Butterfly, and Barney was preparing to do the same in the Zephyr. The Rovers were utterly confounded at this unexpected invasion of their domain, and hastily retreated from the beach.

William Bright, who was the coxswain of the Bluebird, ran her alongside the Zephyr, and took her in tow. In like manner they took possession of the Sylph and the "gondola," leaving the Rovers "alone in their glory," with no means of escaping from the island. With the three boats in tow, they pulled for the beach.

"Now for the Butterfly," said Captain Sedley, as he placed the Sylph in charge of Uncle Ben, and directed William Bright to steer up the lake.

Away dashed the Bluebird. The excited crew had observed the Butterfly about a mile off, pulling towards the river. Tim Bunker, at this safe distance, had paused to observe the movements of the invaders He was as much confounded as Barney had been, and seemed to be at a loss what to do; but when he saw the Bluebird headed towards him, he ordered his crew to pull for the river.

"Steady, boys," said Captain Sedley, when they had approached within a quarter of a mile of the chase. "Probably they will run her ashore and leave her."

But Tim did not mean to do any thing of the kind, and was running the Butterfly directly for the river.

"They will dash her in pieces, I fear," continued the director, when he perceived Tim's intention. 'Pull slowly — put her about, and perhaps they will return."

The Bluebird came round ; but Tim dashed madly on, heedless of the rocks.

"She strikes!" exclaimed Mr. Walker.

"Round again — quick!" added Captain Sedley "They will all be drowned! She fills! There they go!"

The Butterfly had stove a hole in her bow; in an instant she was filled with water, and, careening over, threw her crew into the lake, where they were struggling for life.

"Your boat is stove, Tony," said Captain Sedley to the coxswain of the Butterfly, who had exchanged places with Fred Harper, for the chase.

"Never mind the boat; save the boys!" replied Tony.

"Bravo ! my little hero !" exclaimed Mr. Walker

In a few moments the Bluebird reached the scene of the disaster. The Butterfly was so light that she did not sink ; and most of the Rovers were supporting themselves by holding on at her gunwale. Tim and two or three more had swum ashore, and one would have been drowned, if assistance had not reached him when it did.

The discomfited Rovers were rescued from their perilous situation, and after a severe reprimand, were landed at the nearest shore. Tim made his escape ; but probably none of them have since felt any inclination to imitate the freebooters.

The Butterfly was towed down to her house, and taken out of the water. It was found that two of her planks had been stove, and that the damage could be easily repaired. Mr. Walker proposed sending to Boston for a boat builder ; but Captain Sedley was sure that Uncle Ben, with the assistance of the wheelwright, could repair her quite as well.

The Bluebird then returned to the beach, and the boys were dismissed till three o'clock. The situation of the Rovers on the island was next discussed by Captain Sedley and Mr. Walker, and it was

decided that, as Tim had escaped, it was not expe-
dient to punish his companions, who were less guilty.
So Uncle Ben, with Frank and Tony, was sent off
to bring them ashore. Barney and his band were
glad enough to get off. They freely acknowledged
that they had had enough of "camping out." It
was not what they anticipated. Nearly all of them
had taken severe colds, and since the rain on Monday
night, which had spoiled their provisions, they had
been nearly starved. Barney declared that they
meant to return the boats that night, and if Captain
Sedley would " let them off" this time, they would
never do such a thing again. Like Charles, they had
been punished enough, and with some good advice
they were permitted to depart. How they made
peace with their parents I cannot say ; but probably
many of them "had to take it."   As for Tim Bunker,
he did not show his face in Rippleton again, but
made his way to Boston, where he shipped in a vessel
bound for the East Indies ; and every body in town
was glad to get rid of him.

Thus ended the famous "camping out" of the
Rovers. It was a very pleasant and romantic thing

to think about; but the reality was sufficient to effect a radical cure, and convince them that "yellow-covered books" did not tell the truth.

At three o'clock the boys reassembled, and the crews were organized and officers selected. By a unanimous vote, Frank Sedley was chosen commodore of the fleet. The next morning the Butterfly was repaired, and the squadron made its first voyage round the lake.

But as the rest of the week was occupied in drilling, and the manœuvres were necessarily imperfect, I pass over the time till the August vacation, when the fleet made a grand excursion up Rippleton River.

CHAPTER XIX.

THE CRUISE OF THE FLEET.

THE school year was ended; and it was remarked that the school had never been in a more flourishing condition. The boys, stimulated by the boat organizations, had made remarkable progress, and parents and committee sympathized with them in the pleasant anticipations of the coming vacation.

Since his defection in June, the conduct of Charles Hardy had been in the highest degree satisfactory. His character seemed to be radically changed. He did not "put on airs," nor aspire to high places. His pride had been lowered, and he was modest and gentle; therefore my young friends will not be surprised to learn that his associates had rewarded his endeavors to do well by electing him coxswain of the Zephyr.

On the morning of the day appointed for the

grand excursion, the squadron, as it formed in line opposite Captain Sedley's house, consisted of the following boats, manned and commanded as below : —

Zephyr,	12 oars, (bearing the broad pennant of Commodore Sedley,) . .	Charles Hardy.
Butterfly,	12 oars, ...	Paul Munroe.
Bluebird,	12 "	Fred Harper.
Rainbow,	12 "	William Bright.
Lily,	8 "	Henry Brown.
Dart,	8 "	Dick Chester,
Dip,	4 " (tender,) . .	Tony Weston.

My young readers need not be indignant at finding so brave and skilful an officer as Tony Weston in command of the little Dip, deeming it an insignificant position for him to occupy ; for the tender was to be detailed on special duty, and the appointment was a marked compliment to his skill and judgment.

The system of signals established for the use of the fleet was very simple, and consisted of plain flags of red, white, blue, yellow, green, orange, and purple. each color being a distinct order. The discipline of the fleet was of a mongrel character, composed of

20 *

naval and military tactics. When the squadron sailed in compact order, verbal commands were given; and when the boats were too far apart for the word to be heard, signals were used. But these details will be better understood as the squadron proceeds on its voyage.

The boats were ranged in line, side by side, with the Zephyr on the right, the Butterfly on the left, and the Dip in the middle, each with its gay flags floating to the breeze. All the oars were in-board, and the clubs were waiting for the commodore's orders.

On board the Zephyr, a longer staff than she had formerly used was erected, on which, half way up, was placed her fly, and at the top the broad pennant — of blue, covered with silver stars. On this pole the signals were hoisted, when the pennant had to be lowered for the time.

All eyes were directed to the commodore, who was standing up in the stern sheets of the flag boat.

"Ready!" said he, in a voice loud enough to be heard the whole length of the line; and every boy grasped his oar

"Up!"

It was a beautiful sight to observe the precision with which the oars were erected. A company of soldiers could not have handled their muskets with more unanimity.

"Down!" and in like manner the oars dropped into the water.

Those who have observed the manner in which a military officer gives his orders have discovered the secret of this pleasing concord of action. Commands consist, except in a series, of two words; and dwelling for an instant on the first keeps all in a state of readiness to act the instant the second is given. Frank had studied the matter while witnessing the evolutions of the Rippleton Guards, and he had adopted the plan in the club. When the captain said "shoulder," the men knew what was coming; and at the word "arms," the evolution was performed. So with "present—arms!" "file—right!" "left—wheel!" &c.; and to these observations he was indebted for the proficiency of his club, and of the fleet.

"Ready—pull!" he continued.

The stroke was very slow, and each coxswain was obliged to keep his boat in line with the others, the flag boat regulating their speed.

When the squadron had reached the upper part of the lake, the pennant was dropped, and up went a red flag.

" Cease — rowing ! " said all the coxswains, except the Zephyr's.

Then the red flag was lowered, and a blue one was hoisted.

" In single line," the coxswain of the Bluebird, which was next to the Zephyr, interpreted the signal, and his boat followed the flag.

The others came into the line in proper order, and the squadron passed entirely round the lake.

" Cease — rowing ! " exclaimed the coxswains, in concert, as the red flag again appeared.

Up went a green flag, and the line was formed ; then a yellow, to form in sections of two. In this order the squadron pulled down the lake again, to the widest part, where various fanciful evolutions were performed — which it would be impossible to describe on paper. One of them was rowing in a

circle round the Dip; another was two circles of
three boats each, pulling in opposite directions.
Then the boats were sent off in six different ways,
forming a hexagon, with the tender in the centre;
after which they all came together so that their stems
touched each other, in the shape of a star.

"Now, boys, we are ready for the voyage up Rippleton River," said Commodore Sedley. "I need
not tell you that the utmost caution must be used.
Watch the flags closely, and every coxswain be very
prudent."

"Ay, ay!"

"Tony will lead in the Dip, and each boat will
place a man in the bow to look out for buoys, which
he will place over rocks and shoals."

"Ay, ay," answered the coxswains.

"Now, Tony, you may go up and mark off the
rocks at the mouth of the river."

The little Dip, which had a picked crew for the
occasion, darted away up the lake, leaving the rest
of the fleet to follow.

"Form a line!" shouted Frank, and the boats
backed out from their positions, and in a moment had
obeyed the order.

" Ready — pull ; " and the fleet moved slowly and grandly up the lake.

The boys were in high spirits. There was something inspiring in the operations of the squadron that would have moved a more steady mind than that of a boy of twelve. Every moment was a revelation of the power that dwelt in them, of the beauty of order, of the grace of harmonious action. As in the great world, a single intractable spirit might have produced a heap of confusion, and it was the purpose of the organization to bring each into harmony with the whole.

The fleet reached the mouth of the river. Tony had placed buoys on the dangerous rocks each side of the channel, so that the boats, by approaching it in the right direction, could easily pass through in safety.

The Dip had been provided with a large number of these buoys. They were pieces of board, part of them painted red, and part blue, with a line and weight attached to each. Near the dangerous rock or shoal one of these buoys was to be located, which would be kept in place by the weight. The coxswains had written instructions from the commodore to keep red ones on the starboard side, and blue on the port side, going up the river, and *vice versa* coming down.

The Zephyr took position near the rocks to see that every boat approached the channel in the right direction, as, if they did not, they would be sure to strike. By these extraordinary precautions, the fleet passed through in safety, and three stunning cheers announced that the passage had been effected.

" Here we are, Charley," said Frank, as the Zephyr pulled ahead of the other boats.

" All safe, thanks to the skill and prudence of our commodore," replied Charles ; and the reader will be struck with the modesty of his language.

" Where is Tony ? I don't see him."

" Round the bend, I guess ; but here are his buoys all along."

" Signal man, hoist the blue," continued the commodore ; and the fleet followed in single line.

" Here's the bridge ; I fancy Tony knows the soundings here," said Charles.

" Ay, there is the rock on which Mr. Walker's chaise hung. It is almost out of water, now."

" Did you hear what Mr. Walker said when some one asked him why he did not sue the town ? "

" No ; what was it ? "

" He said it was the luckiest day of his life when he pitched off the bridge."

" Indeed ! "

" He has thought so much better of humanity since, and it introduced him to Tony Weston, whom he calls a hero in embryo."

" Mr. Walker is a nice man — a whole-souled man."

" That he is ! How many men would have done for us what he did ? And I, in particular, have reason to be grateful to him," said Charles, with a sigh. " I shall never forget him and your father, wherever my lot is cast."

" That is manly of you, Charley. But I am sure they have been abundantly rewarded by your devotion to duty since."

" I have tried to do right."

" You have done well ; every body says so."

" I cannot soon forget what a fool I was to believe Tim's wicked lies. I suppose I wanted to believe them, or I should not."

" It is a great pity we ever let Tim into the club ; but we meant right ; we meant to reform him. Where do you suppose he is now ? "

" Some where near the Cape of Good Hope."

" My father thinks he has got enough of the sea by this time."

" I dare say. Didn't you ever feel a desire to go to sea, Frank ? "

"No; not lately."

" Nor I ; Tim Bunker lent me the Red Corsair of the Caribbean Sea, just before that scrape, and I thought then that I should like to take a voyage."

" My father will not let me read such books ; and since he had told me what they are, and what their influence is, I don't want to read them."

" There's Tony, with the red flag hoisted."

The red flag had been agreed upon as the signal to stop the fleet, when the navigation was very hazardous, or impracticable.

" Cease — rowing ! " said Charles.

Frank ordered his signal man to hoist the red in the flag boat.

21

"Can't we go any farther than this?" asked Charles.

"I don't know; we are not more than a mile above the bridge."

"Here comes the Dip."

"Well, Tony, what's the matter?" said the commodore, as the tender approached.

"I haven't found a clear channel yet. The bed of the river is covered with rocks," replied Tony, as the Dip came alongside the Zephyr.

"Then we must call this the head of navigation," added Frank, with a laugh, though he was not a little disappointed to find the cruise up so soon.

"Perhaps not; there is water enough, but the twelve-oar boats are so long they can hardly dodge the rocks. The Lily and the Dart can get through very well."

"Have you sounded clear across?"

"I haven't had time to examine very thoroughly yet. If you let the boats lay off, I will look farther."

"Very well; I will go with you in the Dart," replied the commodore, as he ordered up a white and

a blue flag, which was the signal for the Dart to
close up.

The signal was obeyed, and Frank followed the
Dip. After half an hour's search, a clear channel
was found close to the land ; so close that the oars
could not be used, and a party was sent on shore to
drag them through with ropes.

The line was formed again, and the squadron
slowly followed the Dip as she examined the river
For the next mile there were no obstructions.

" Twelve o'clock ! " shouted Fred Harper from the
Bluebird.

" Dinner time, then," replied Frank. " Here is a
beautiful grove, and we will land and dine. Hoist
the orange " — the signal to land.

CHAPTER XX.

THE HOSPITALITIES OF OAKLAWN.

THE boys all had remarkably good appetites, and therefore dinner was no unimportant event in the experience of the day. Somehow, boys contrive to be hungry at almost all times of the day, even without the stimulus of pulling three hours at an oar. There was something, too, in the circumstance of dining in a beautiful grove, on the bank of the river, with their boats floating near them, which rendered the occasion peculiarly pleasant — which made their cold meat, doughnuts, and apple pie taste much better than usual.

But the adventure was not yet completed. The head waters of navigation had not been reached, and their love of exploring did not permit them to spend any unnecessary time over the meal. Tony and his oarsmen had reported themselves at the grove, and after "bolting" their dinner, had resumed their occupation; and the boys perceived the Dip half a mile up the river before they were ready to start.

"All aboard!" said Frank; and the crews, hastily gathering up their tin pails and their baskets, tumbled into the boats.

The Zephyr led off, followed by the other boats of the squadron.

"I see no buoys ahead," said Frank, after they had advanced some distance. "The navigation must be unobstructed."

"It looks like deep water," answered Charles.

"And Tony's crew are pulling very hard; they are going faster than we do."

"He is trying to gain time against he reaches a bad place. There he goes round a bend. Were you ever up here before, Frank?"

"I have been to Oaklawn, which is about four miles from Rippleton. Of course I never came up the river."

"Wouldn't it be fine if we could get up to Oaklawn?"

"Perhaps we can."

21 *

"This is smooth work," continued Frank.　Can't we give a little variety to the excursion?"

"What?"

"Hoist the yellow, signalman," replied the commodore.　"We will pull a while in sections of two, and sing some songs."

Obedient to the signal, the boats of the fleet came into the order prescribed, and the boys waked up the hills and the woods with the earnestness of their song.　It was a beautiful and cheering sight to see them gliding over the clear waters, while their voices mingled with those of the songsters which nature had given to the hill-side and the forest.　Their hearts were glad, and in beautiful unison with the scene around them.

"Rapids!" exclaimed Frank, when the boat reached the bend.　"Up with the blue!"

"Steady!" added Charles.　"Pull slowly."

"Tony has been very busy," continued Frank, pointing to the buoys, that speckled the waters.　I am afraid the cruise is about up."

"Tony has passed the rapids.　You know steamboats go down the rapids on the St. Lawrence River."

" Ah, there is Oaklawn," said Frank, pointing to the spire of a church in the distance. " We cannot go much farther, I know."

" We have made nearly four miles."

What the commodore had styled " rapids " were not a very formidable difficulty. Near one bank was a ledge of rocks, over which the waters dashed with considerable energy ; but though there was the same descent on the other side, no obstruction appeared to check them from attempting the passage. Tony had accomplished it, and had left no warning to deter them.

" Shall we go through, Frank ? "

" Ay ; bend on sharp, and she will leap up like a fawn. Now for it ! "

The Zephyrs applied all their strength to the oars, and the boat darted up the rapids with no other detriment than taking in two or three pailfuls of water.

The rest of the fleet followed, with the exception of the Lily, without accident ; and she, not having sufficient headway, was carried down again. By the skill of her coxswain, however, she was saved from damage, and her second attempt was successful.

The navigation was again tolerably safe, and for half a mile they proceeded on their way withou interruption.

" There's a bridge," said Charles, pointing ahead.

" And there is the Dip, with the red hoisted Tony seems to have given it up." He has made fast to the bridge."

On the shore was a crowd of men and boys, who were holding a parley with the pilot of the expedition ; but when they saw the squadron approaching they seemed petrified with astonishment. The boys thrust their hands deep in their trousers' pockets, and with mouths wide open stared in speechless wonder. The arrival of Columbus on the shores of the new world could not have been more astounding to the natives than was the coming of the Wood Lake squadron to the boys of Oaklawn.

" Sheer off, Charley, to the port side of the river, and we will come into line. The river is wide enough here, I believe. Up with the green ! "

On dashed the boats in the rear till they came into the line. The river widened into a kind of pond ; but the line stretched clear across it — making a very imposing appearance.

"Slowly; cease — rowing!" continued Frank.
"Ready — up!" and the sixty-eight oars of the
fleet glittered in the sunshine before the astonished
Oaklawners, who were gathering in great numbers
on the shore and bridge.

"Well, Tony, the cruise is up," said Frank, when
the Dip came into line.

"Yes," replied the pilot, pointing under the bridge,
where the river dashed its foaming waters down a
long reach of half-exposed rocks. "'We can't get
over those."

"No; and we may as well land, and take a look
at Oaklawn. Hoist the orange. Ready — down!"

Each boat landed its crew at a convenient place,
and they were then marshalled into a procession.
They were formed in sections of four, each crew pre-
ceded by its coxswain, with one of the flags on each
side of him. The commodore marched at the head
of the company, and in this order they proceeded
through the principal street of the village. Of course
their appearance excited a great deal of wonder and
not a little admiration. Several of the principal
citizens, unwilling that their guests should depart

unwelcomed, got up an *impromptu* reception, and the clubs were invited to the Town Hall, where some very pretty speeches were made by the chairman of the Selectmen, of the School Committee, the representative to the General Court, and other distinguished individuals; to whom the commodore replied with a great deal of dignity and self-possession.

While the speeches were proceeding, the ladies were not idle; and the boys were next invited to a collation on the green; after which they marched back to the river, and reëmbarked. Three times three cheers were given for the people of Oaklawn, and the word was given to pull for home.

The boys of the village were not so ready to part with them, and some twenty of them followed the boats, on the bank of the river.

" I say, Frank, these folks were very kind to us," Charles remarked.

" They were, indeed."

" And the boys seem to enjoy it."

" I suppose not many of them ever saw our boats before."

" Suppose we take them in; they will be very

willing to walk home, say from the grove where we dined, for the sake of the sail."

"Good! I didn't think of that before. Up with the orange!"

The boats landed, and the astonished Oaklawn boys were distributed among them. They seemed to regard the favor as an unexpected condescension, and their delight knew no bounds. As Little Paul expressed it, "they were tickled half to death;" and when they reached the grove, it was a sad and bitter disappointment for them to get out and go home.

"I was thinking of something," said Charles, a little while after they had landed their passengers.

"What was it, Charley?" replied the commodore.

"That we might invite the boys of Oaklawn to spend a day with us on the lake."

"Capital!"

"We could give them a picnic on Centre Island."

"We will do it; and now that we know the river we can easily come up as far as the grove after them."

"Or up to the rapids; there is no danger this side of them."

This plan was discussed in all its details, and every thing was agreed upon by the time they reached the lake. The passage down the river had been much quicker than the upward trip, and before sunset the boats were all housed, and the clubs had separated.

On the following week the courtesies of the fleet were extended to the boys of Oaklawn, as arranged by the commodore, and a very fine time they had of it. Their guests, numbering over forty, were entertained in every conceivable manner — the day's sports concluding with a grand race, in which all the boats were entered, and in which the Butterfly won the honors.

A new programme was made up every week during the vacation. Lighthouses were built, channels surveyed, shores charted; indeed, every thing which the ingenuity of the boys could devise was brought forward to add fresh interest to the sports of the lake.

And thus the season passed away, and winter came again. The fleet was laid up, and the useful and pleasant recreations of the club rooms were

substituted for the active excitement of boating
Lectures were given, essays were read, debates held,
every week; and the progress of the boys out of
school, as well as within, was highly satisfactory to
all concerned.

CHAPTER XXI.

CONCLUSION.

I SUPPOSE, as the present volume completes the history of the Boat Club, that my young readers will wish to know something of the subsequent fortunes of the prominent characters of the association. It gives me pleasure to say, that not one of them has been recreant to his opportunities, or abandoned his high standard of character; that the moral, mental, and physical discipline of the organization has proved salutary in the highest degree. The members of the boat clubs are now active members of society. Each is pulling an oar, or steering his bark, on the great ocean of life. Some are in humble spheres, as in the little Dip; others are in more extended fields, as in the majestic twelve-oar boats.

Frank Sedley is a lawyer. His father has gone to enjoy his reward in the world beyond the grave;

and Frank, who was married a year ago to Mary Weston, resides in the mansion by the lake. His brilliant talents and unspotted integrity have elevated him to a respectable position, for one so young, in the legal profession; and there is no doubt but that he will arrive at eminence in due time.

Uncle Ben is still alive, and continues to dwell at the mansion of the Sedleys. The boats are still in being, and are manned by the boys belonging to the school — under the direction of the veteran.

Tony Weston is a merchant. At the age of seventeen he was taken into the counting room of Mr. Walker, and at twenty-one admitted as an equal partner. The man is what the boy was — noble, generous, kind.

Strange as it may seem, only one boy of the whole number has become a sailor. Fred Harper went to sea when he left school, and was recently appointed master of a fine clipper ship, bound for India. Little Paul is a journeyman carpenter. He is in a humble sphere, but none the less respected on that account. His father, who recovered his health, paid the notes he had made to the clubs. The money was applied to the purchase of books and a philosophical apparatus, which rendered the winter evenings of the clubs still more attractive.

'Squire Chase "worked out his destiny" in Rippleton, and finally was so thoroughly despised that he found it convenient to leave the place. Perhaps my readers will be a little surprised when I tell them that Charles Hardy is a minister of the gospel. He was recently settled in a small town in Connecticut. The boat club changed his character, — purged it of the evil, and confirmed the good, — and he is now a humble and devoted laborer in the vineyard of the Master.

Wood Lake is still beautiful, and the remembrances of former days are still lovingly cherished by Frank and Tony, who reside on its banks. The Zephyr and Butterfly, though somewhat battered and worm eaten, are occasionally seen, near the close of day, with a lady and gentleman in the stern sheets of each. The youthful crews are happier than usual, for one bears the ex-commodore and lady, and the other the hero of Rippleton Bridge and his lady.